"Sometimes things happen and we're forced into doing things we might not do otherwise."

Zoe's son thought about that for a moment. "Like you had to start baby-sitting and rent the cabin because you need more money to help pay the bills since Dad isn't here."

"Right," said Zoe around the lump in her throat. Chris was too young to have to worry about their finances.

"Don't cry, Mom."

"What makes you think I'm going to cry?"

"Your voice is all funny and your eyes are all shiny."

Zoe's heart gave a painful lurch. Was renting the cabin to a single man the right thing to do? Was she setting them up for a fall?

Still…she'd never known just how starved they were for a man in their lives until now.

She'd had no idea how starved *she* was for a man's attention.

Dear Reader,

Well, the wait is over—*New York Times* bestselling author Diana Palmer is back, and Special Edition has got her! In *Carrera's Bride*, another in Ms. Palmer's enormously popular LONG, TALL TEXANS miniseries, an innocent Jacobsville girl on a tropical getaway finds herself in need of protection—and gets it from an infamous casino owner who is not all that he appears! I think you'll find this one was well worth the wait….

We're drawing near the end of our in-series continuity THE PARKS EMPIRE. This month's entry is *The Marriage Act* by Elissa Ambrose, in which a shy secretary learns that her one night of sleeping with the enemy has led to unexpected consequences. Next up is *The Sheik & the Princess Bride* by Susan Mallery, in which a woman hired to teach a prince how to fly finds herself *his* student, as well, as he gives her lessons…in love! In *A Baby on the Ranch*, part of Stella Bagwell's popular MEN OF THE WEST miniseries, a single mother-to-be finds her long-lost family—and, just possibly, the love of her life. And a single man in the market for household help finds himself about to take on the role of husband—and father of four—in Penny Richards's *Wanted: One Father*. Oh, and speaking of single parents—a lonely widow with a troubled adolescent son finds the solution to both her problems in her late husband's law-enforcement partner, in *The Way to a Woman's Heart* by Carol Voss.

So enjoy, and come back next month for six wonderful selections from Silhouette Special Edition.

Happy Thanksgiving!

Gail Chasan
Senior Editor

Please address questions and book requests to:
Silhouette Reader Service
U.S.: 3010 Walden Ave., P.O. Box 1325, Buffalo, NY 14269
Canadian: P.O. Box 609, Fort Erie, Ont. L2A 5X3

Wanted:
One Father
PENNY RICHARDS

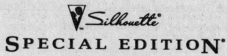

SPECIAL EDITION

Published by Silhouette Books

America's Publisher of Contemporary Romance

For the ladies of the Round Ball Café—
Mary, Jayne and Dot.

Thanks for listening and for the ideas.

 SILHOUETTE BOOKS

ISBN 0-373-24649-8

WANTED: ONE FATHER

Copyright © 2004 by Penny Richards

PENNY RICHARDS

also has written under the pseudonym Bay Matthews and has been writing for Silhouette for sixteen years. She's been a cosmetologist, an award-winning artist and worked briefly as an interior decorator. She also served a brief stint as a short-order cook in her daughter-in-law's café. Claiming everything interests her, she collects dolls, books and antiques and loves movies, reading, cooking, catalogs, redoing old houses, learning how to do anything new, Jeff Bridges, music by Yanni, poetry by Rod McKuen, yard sales and flea markets (she loves finding a bargain), gardening (she's a Master Gardener) and baseball. She has three children and nine grandchildren and lives in Arkansas with her husband of thirty-six years in a soon-to-be-one-hundred-year-old Queen Anne house listed on the National Register of Historic Places. She supports and works with her local garden club, arts league, literacy council and Friends of the Library. Always behind, she dreams of simplifying her life. Unfortunately, another deadline looms and there is paper to be hung and baseboards to refinish....

Chapter One

Words to the scene he should be writing for his newest novel unfolded in Max Murdock's mind as he negotiated the last block to his mother's house. A part of him knew he was driving too fast for the neighborhood streets, but he was late picking up Annabelle, as he had been every night this week. Pulling into the driveway, he shut off the SUV's engine, flung open the door and ran up the steps. His hand was inches from the knob when the front door opened and he stood face-to-face with his mother. Donna Fielding had the determined look in her eyes that said he was about to hear something he didn't want to hear. Normally an easygoing woman, she was hard to ruffle, but when she did get her dander up, it was enough to make even a grown man quake. Some things never changed.

He couldn't help being late. The work on his book

had gone exceptionally well that afternoon, and he'd needed to take advantage of the burst of inspiration— an infrequent visitor in the past few months. In fact, since he'd started his second book, a psychological thriller set in New Orleans, the flashes of genius had been few and far between. Max wasn't sure if his difficulty arose from the pressure to make this book as good as his first, or if it was the result of the major changes that had happened in his life. His wife had deserted him eight months earlier, which had led to a divorce and Max being granted custody of Annabelle.

Weighed down by a considerable amount of guilt over his tardiness, he brushed past his mother and began gathering Annabelle's things, reaching for a stuffed rabbit with one hand and gently trying to pry a slobber-soaked book from his eleven-month-old daughter's wet fist with his other. Annabelle wasn't going for it. The moment he took the book from her, she let out a screech guaranteed to send any inexperienced father's heart plummeting. His mom claimed that Annabelle had his temper, a theory Max didn't want to accept. Wherever she'd gotten it, it was a force to be reckoned with when she didn't get her way. New to fatherhood, he had no idea how to cope and was more inclined to try to appease her, which meant he usually gave in to her emotional blackmail. Like now. Without even being aware that he was doing so, he handed the book back. The screaming stopped immediately.

"Max, we need to talk."

Annabelle poked a corner of the dripping book back into her mouth. Totally defeated by the eighteen pounds of future womanhood who sat staring up at him with solemn dark eyes that bore no trace of tears, Max raked a hand through his hair and turned his own brown eyes to his mother. He was definitely in trouble. As with his daughter, it was best to admit his faults, give in, do whatever it took to keep his mom happy. At this point in his life, she was the only person he knew without a doubt he could count on. To alienate her would be disaster.

"I know I'm late again, Mom," he began in a conciliatory tone as he stuffed a container of wipes into Annabelle's diaper bag. "But the book was going really well, and when the muse is sitting on my shoulder, it's hard to stop."

"I don't mind that you were late, Max," Donna Fielding said, "but—"

"And I know I'm an inconsiderate jerk," he interrupted, not even hearing that he'd been absolved of the sin of tardiness. "I take advantage of you, and—"

"Yes, you do," Donna said with a nod, taking her own turn at interruption.

Max blinked. He hadn't expected her to agree with him.

"Sit down, son," she said in a gentle voice. "I need to talk to you."

Panic flared. What was so important that he had to sit before she could tell him? She was getting older, and… "What's wrong?" he asked, his worried gaze meeting hers.

Donna smiled. "Nothing to make you look like that. It's just that Paul and I have been talking, and there are some things he wants to do…" Her voice trailed away. "This is so hard, darn it." She took a deep breath and looked him squarely in the eyes. "I hate to break it to you this way, honey, but you're going to have to find someone else to take care of Annabelle."

For the second time in as many minutes, Max's heart plummeted. There was no one he knew who could watch Annabelle while he worked. The idea of trying to combine child care and writing was something he couldn't begin to comprehend. All he could think to say was, "Why?"

"Paul has always wanted to travel, but since he retired I've been keeping Annabelle for you, so our plans were put on hold. Neither of us minded for the short term, but we aren't getting any younger. As much as I want to help you, and as much as I know you need me, I feel that my first priority should be my husband."

Max knew she was right. It was a lesson he'd learned the hard way from the breakdown of his own marriage. Paul Fielding was a great guy, and he'd been a good provider for Max, his brother and their mother after his dad passed away when Max was twelve. Paul deserved to spend his retirement the way he wanted. Max told his mother so.

"I knew you'd understand," she said. "And I'm so sorry to let you down this way."

"You aren't letting me down, Mom," he assured her. "I knew you couldn't keep Annabelle indefinitely."

"It may take a while, but you'll find a good sitter. There are a lot of excellent day care places here."

Here was Hot Springs, the place he'd moved to eight months earlier when his wife, Cara, had packed up while he was at physical therapy for a bullet wound he'd sustained as a Little Rock cop. She'd left their then three-month-old daughter with a neighbor and Max a brief, handwritten note saying she was sorry, but it had been a mistake. All of it. She should never have married him, hating his work as a policeman the way she did. She should never have stayed with him for five miserable years, should never have thought bringing a baby into the world would somehow miraculously mend their decaying marriage. The love was long gone, and she wasn't very good mother material.

He shook his head, uncertain if he was trying to dislodge the troubling memories or answer his mother. "I can't leave Annabelle in a day care."

His mother smiled and laid a comforting hand on his arm. "Honey. People do it every day."

"I want her to grow up in a home environment."

"Then I'm sure you'll be able to find someone to come to the house to keep her," Donna said.

Max shook his head again. "You know I can't work with someone in the house. There would be too many distractions and if I want to keep a roof over our heads, I have to meet this deadline."

Donna gave a little shrug. "Well, then look for someone who keeps children in her home."

Yeah. But how?

As if she read his mind, his mother said, "Check the newspaper and see what's available. Then set up some interviews."

"How will I know if the person is right or not?"

"I don't suppose there's any way you can ever know for sure, but you're an ex-cop, Max, and you've always had good instincts. Use them."

"You make it sound easy."

"Trust me, honey, it will be okay."

"So how long do I have before you and Paul take off?"

"Two weeks?" Donna said, with a questioning lift of her eyebrows.

Max nodded in resignation. "Fair enough."

He kissed his mother goodbye, assuring her that her decision was the right one. He loaded Annabelle and her things into his SUV and drove home, damning Cara's selfishness and his own feelings of inadequacy. She'd had it all worked out—from her perspective, anyway. There was little Max could do but pick up the remnants of his life and see if he could manage to make it whole again.

To be honest, he had come to the conclusion that Cara was right. Their marriage was all wrong, had been from the start. He realized now that he would never have been able to please her, no matter what he did. So here he was, one baby to care and provide for, and one book to deliver in two months. No. Make that one better-than-excellent book to deliver. Thanks to the success of his first endeavor, he was under the gun to produce a knockout second novel.

He pulled into the driveway of the house he was leasing and turned toward the back to look at Annabelle, who was still chewing on the book. "So what do you think, Annabelle? Got any ideas about who we can get to watch you?"

As if she understood what he'd said, she took the book from her mouth, held it out like a peace offering and said, "Da da."

Max's stomach knotted at the thought of being responsible for her 24/7. He needed help—fast.

Zoe Barlow sat on the front porch of her eighty-year old farmhouse situated on forty acres ten miles south of Hot Springs, a sweating glass of iced tea in her hand, watching her three boys at play. She had one sandaled foot tucked beneath her, while the other pushed the glider in a soothing back-and-forth motion. An errant spring breeze teased a strand of auburn hair from the untidy twist clipped to the top of her head. Distractedly, she reached up her free hand and pushed it back. The boys were playing Frisbee with Mutt, the young mongrel dog someone had dumped near the farm a few days before Christmas. When they had begged her to keep him overnight because it was snowing and he was cold and shivering and "so cute," she'd agreed. The next morning, they'd asked if they could keep him—after all, he was "free." By that time Zoe realized that the dog was sick, and she'd been conscience-bound to take him to the vet while she "thought about it." Three-and-a-half months and two hundred dollars later, the "free" dog was still with them, as much a part of the family as any one of the boys.

"I didn't realize he'd get so big," Zoe said, turning a troubled blue gaze to Celia Bell, her neighbor and best friend, who sat in the rocking chair next to the glider. "I certainly had no idea he'd eat so much."

"Who?" Celia asked, frowning.

"Mutt."

"Oh."

For several minutes, neither woman spoke. The sound of the children's laughter was punctuated by the occasional bark of the dog and the squeak of the glider's mechanism.

"Dr. Gardner says Mike needs his tonsils out as soon as possible."

Celia gave a philosophical shrug. "He'll feel better when he gets them out."

"And Chris is going to have to have braces." Zoe

watched her oldest son throw the Frisbee. Mutt grabbed it, but instead of obeying the command to take it to Chris, he began running the other way. The boys gave chase, laughing and yelling. Zoe sighed. "And he's going to have to be neutered."

"Who, Chris?"

Zoe turned to Celia in surprise. Then, realizing her friend hadn't followed her train of thought, she laughed. Seconds later, concern banished the smile from Zoe's lips and leached it from her eyes. "I don't know how I'm going to pay for it all," she said.

"You'll manage. You have insurance, don't you?"

"Yeah," Zoe said with a nod and a lift of her shoulders. "It isn't very good insurance. The deductible is outrageous, but it was the only way I could afford anything. Even as an outpatient, Mike's surgery is going to cost me an arm and leg."

"I've tried not to be nosy, but didn't David leave you anything?"

Zoe's husband, David, had died three years earlier of a virus he'd picked up while donating his time and medical expertise to help children in a small South American village. Being widowed at twenty-nine had been devastating, both emotionally and financially.

"He had a life insurance policy, but by the time I got him home and buried and paid off all his government loans, it didn't leave nearly enough. I used part of what was left to buy this place, thinking it would be a cheap way to live. I invested the rest. I've been living on the interest, but with the economy like it is, that doesn't amount to much. Lately, it never seems to be enough."

"That's why you took a job as a waitress at the catfish place at night."

"Right." Zoe sighed. "The problem with being a waitress is you never know how much you'll make."

"You'll just have to make arrangements to make monthly payments."

Zoe's troubled gaze met Celia's. "I suppose, but I wish there was some way I could make a few extra bucks."

"Art lessons?" Celia suggested.

Zoe, who'd once studied art, supplemented her income with pressed-flower pictures that she sold at local craft fairs. "I thought about that, but I haven't painted since David died, and I'm not sure that would be a good idea with the kids getting out of school in a couple of months. Can you imagine me trying to corral the boys while teaching an art class? No telling what would happen."

Celia cast Zoe a considering look. "Have you given any serious thought to remarrying? Preferably someone filthy rich and, as my mom used to say, 'One foot in the grave, the other on a banana peel?'"

Zoe laughed. "My mom used to say that, too. It's been years since I heard it. And actually, I have thought about the possibility. And the probability."

"That's progress. Even a year ago, you said it was out of the question."

"Funny how time changes things, isn't it?" Zoe asked. "I still love David. A part of me always will. But I've realized I'm young, and that I have a lot of time ahead of me—God willing. I don't want to spend all those years alone." She sighed. "The reality is I never go places to meet eligible men."

"That can be fixed. Once word gets out that you're in the market for a man, all your well-meaning friends will want to introduce you to every widower and divorcé they know."

Zoe gave a wry smile. "That's what scares me. And let's say I did find a man I was attracted to. How many men out there would have the means or desire to take on a wife, three boys and a mongrel dog? He'd have to be little insane. Or a saint."

"It happens every day," Celia said. "So there must be a lot of crazy guys or saints out there."

"I guess." Despite her friend's encouragement, Zoe wasn't convinced. A niggling sense of panic fluttered deep inside her at the thought of spending the rest of her life alone.

"Since there are no nice, nearly dead eligible bachelors on your immediate horizon, have you thought about keeping kids here at the house?"

"Baby-sit?" Zoe asked in surprise.

"Why not? You have the perfect place for kids to run and romp, and the house is certainly big enough when they do have to be inside."

"Hmm," Zoe said. "I never thought of baby-sitting."

"And you could always rent out the cabin."

"Rent the cabin?" Zoe shook her head. "I'm not sure it's fit for human habitation."

"When was the last time you looked at it?"

"When I first bought the farm. There hasn't been any need to check it out since then. I thought it might be a good place for the boys to hang out when they got older and wanted to get away from me, but other than that, I haven't given it much thought."

"Well, think about it now."

"I am," Zoe said. Despite herself, she felt a glimmer of excitement.

"If there is any fixing up to do, Tom can handle the repairs as long as they aren't too major. A little soap, water and paint will probably go a long way," Celia added.

"You may have hit on something," Zoe said as she leaped to her feet. Just as quickly, she plopped back down.

"What?"

"Who's going to want to live this far out?"

"A lot of people. We did, didn't we?"

"Yeah," Zoe said, brightening once again. "There have to be other people who like peace and quiet."

A shrill scream and a round of barking and laughter from the boys and Mutt filled the air.

"Yeah," Celia agreed, smiling. "A little peace and quiet is always good."

"Down you go, sweet thing," Max said softly, laying Annabelle in her crib and handing her the stuffed rabbit she seemed to favor. She reached out to take the plush animal and thanked him with a brief smile which showed off her four front teeth. She was usually such a solemn baby that the smile caught him off guard and stole his breath. Unaccountably pleased, he smiled back at her. She really was a beautiful baby. She looked a lot like the pictures of Cara at the same age, which meant his daughter would no doubt grow up to be a heart-breaker, just like her mother. Max pushed the thought away, laid Annabelle down and tucked a lightweight blanket over her.

He realized with a start that she was growing at an alarming rate. She'd started walking a month ago, and it was becoming harder and harder to keep her in her playpen in the evenings while he did the things he had to do to keep their lives going. Things like laundry, cleaning, cooking. His mom claimed that Annabelle was starting to say a few words, but so far she hadn't felt the inclination to show off to him, except for the one instance a week ago when he'd ask her about a possible baby-sitter and she'd said da da. He figured that had been coincidence. It might be nice when she learned to talk, he thought. At least they could carry on a conversation of sorts and she could let her wants and needs be known instead of forcing him to guess at the source of her tears. Smiling at the thought, he chucked her under the chin. "Good night. Sleep tight. Don't let the bedbugs bite."

Annabelle answered with another of those unexpected smiles. Max felt his chest swell with a strange and unexpected emotion that left him disconcerted and bewildered. He turned and left the room, grateful that all it took to get Annabelle to sleep was a full tummy. She'd given up her pacifier at eight months, and, thanks to his mom, he'd never gotten into the habit of giving her a bottle in bed. He just put her into the crib and cranked up either the mobile that was sufficiently out of her reach or the nifty gizmo that flashed images onto the ceiling. She watched until she went to sleep.

Like Cara, Max had come to the conclusion that he wasn't very good parent material. He'd asked himself a hundred times the past eight months why the two of them had even considered having a baby. All Annabelle's birth had done was add another layer of tension to their lives. But unlike Cara, Max wasn't one to walk out when things got bad. Mistake or not, Annabelle was his child, and he knew he was responsible for her life…in more ways than one. He would do his best by her, and that included finding a baby-sitter who would give her the kind of care he felt she deserved, care he was totally unequipped to give her himself.

She'd made him nervous from the first, but Cara had been there to take care of most of Annabelle's needs. When Cara left, Annabelle was still so tiny, so fragile. Max felt as if he were some clumsy giant trying to handle a piece of delicate porcelain. He'd tried to carry his weight as much as his work would allow when he and Cara were together, but with her gone, there was so much more to do. If it wasn't time to feed her, she needed changing. And there was the crying. Lots of crying.

To add insult to injury, his daughter seemed to know somehow that he was in over his head, increasing his feelings of inadequacy. There were more times than he could count when he'd done everything he could possibly think of, but Annabelle would not stop crying. But his mother, answering his SOS, could pick Annabelle up and she'd quiet almost instantly.

His nerves were shot; he'd started biting his nails, something he hadn't done since he was a kid. He thought about taking up smoking again, a habit he'd given up during Cara's pregnancy. Writing anything even remotely coherent became an impossibility. After a week of trying to juggle his writing and taking care of Annabelle, his mother had agreed to keep her for a while.

She kept telling him that Annabelle reacted the way she did to him because she *did* sense his nervousness. If he would only stay calm, things would be different. But he couldn't imagine *calm* in connection with Annabelle. She scared him silly, and that was a fact. He dreaded picking her up from his mom's, dreaded the time he spent with her by himself. He couldn't sleep for fear she'd stop breathing during the night. He was afraid she'd choke if he gave her a teething biscuit, afraid she'd slip out of his grip when he bathed her, afraid he'd accidentally give her too much medicine when she was sick. Afraid, period. He, honored as rookie of the year, a detective with numerous collars and a fair share of citations to his credit, was scared spitless of an eleven-month-old baby with a mop of curly brown hair, dark eyes and a Cupid's bow mouth.

Lately, when Annabelle was down for the night, Max sat on his back patio with a glass of tea, watching the squirrels play and the birds splash in the concrete bird-bath. It was a ritual he enjoyed almost every evening now that the weather was warm enough. It was the only time he felt he could truly relax. But relaxing was far from his mind tonight. His two weeks were disappearing rapidly, and he still hadn't found anyone to take his mother's place. It was time to get cracking. He was beginning to feel panic gnawing at the edge of his composure, a situation he did his best to conceal from everyone, including Annabelle, who seemed able to hone in on his moods like radar on a plane in a no-fly zone.

Knowing he couldn't put the task off any longer, Max showered, pulled on a pair of shorts and a T-shirt and went to the kitchen to get a cola from the refrigerator. After popping the top, he settled himself on the sofa and opened the Saturday *Sentinel Record* with a feeling of dread.

That first night he'd checked the paper, he'd talked

to no less than five women who'd advertised their services. He'd even gone so far as to go to the houses of four of them, but hadn't felt right with any of them.

What are you looking for, Murdock? A clone of your mom? Wouldn't that be nice? *Well, you ain't gonna find her, so you may as well lower your standards a little.*

Maybe that was it. His standards were too high. It was unlikely he'd be able to find a woman who would put Annabelle's wants and needs ahead of her own children's, or those of other children she kept. Highly unlikely that he'd locate a paragon who'd not only baby-sit but send a casserole home with him when he picked up Annabelle. Even less likely that his frequent tardiness would be disregarded with a shrug and a kiss of forgiveness. He supposed that the best he could hope for was someone who would treat Annabelle with fairness and kindness.

With a sigh, Max opened the paper to the classified section and found the ads for baby-sitting at home. There were several new ones since he'd last looked. Maybe he'd get lucky. He zeroed in on the first ad.

Spacious farmhouse in the country, big yard, home cooked meals, other children and friendly dog to play with.

The ad had been in that first day he'd looked. It was the only one Max hadn't called, because it said nothing about the person's qualifications. Did this woman— whoever she was—think that a big yard made up for lack of competence? As he had before, he put a big *X* through the ad and went on to the next one.

Christian woman, mother of two, would like to keep your precious little one. Six years' day care experience. References provided.

Now that was more like it—at least the woman gave some information. Max picked up the phone and dialed the number. Two minutes into the conversation, the woman was trying to convert him, instead of talking about what she could do for Annabelle. He thanked her for her time and made another *X* on the paper. He called the five others who were listed, hoping against hope that he'd hear something in the feminine voices to convince him that *this* one was the right one.

It didn't happen. One woman sounded about fifteen. One sounded harsh. One seemed downright stupid. One was too interested in how she would be paid, since he didn't have a regular nine-to-five job. The last one sounded so old he knew she couldn't keep up with his soon-to-be running daughter. Frowning and fighting a growing feeling of frustration, he glared at the paper as if his fierce determination and greater need might cause it to suddenly offer some sort of guidance.

Spacious farmhouse in the country, big yard, home cooked meals, other children and friendly dog to play with.

Max read the ad three times before he finally sighed in resignation. What the heck, he thought, punching in the number. In another day or two, he would be approaching desperation. Never let it be said that he left a single stone unturned in his search.

"Mom! Can I have a cookie?" seven-year-old Mike yelled, bursting through the back door with its old-fashioned spring. The door slammed shut so hard the entire house seemed to rattle. Zoe, who was on the phone, glanced at the clock on the wall and realized it was getting close to supper time. It seemed impossible that she'd been on the phone for thirty minutes with a woman who'd answered her newspaper ad for a baby-sitter. Zoe cautioned Mike with a "quiet" finger to her lips, then made a sign that he could have just one cookie.

Taking advantage of the fact that she couldn't do much bodily harm while she was on the phone, Mike reached for the cookie jar, grabbed a handful of Snickerdoodles and left by the way he'd come, sneaking a look at his mother and giving her an elfin grin. The door snapped shut with another deafening slam as the phone beeped, alerting Zoe to the fact that someone else was trying to call on the other line. She didn't mind putting friends and family on hold, but this was a possible job. Whoever it was could just call back. Zoe pressed her lips together in frustration and did her best to focus on what the woman was saying. She was clearly concerned about the other children her daughter would be playing with.

"Yes, I know the children should learn to be respectful when I'm on the phone, but I'm having a little trouble with that one," she said into the mouthpiece as she paced the length of her spacious kitchen. She opened the refrigerator door and peered inside. What could she fix for dinner that was fast and nutritious that the boys would eat? Her heart fell when she realized not much fit that bill. "I have three boys, ages ten, seven and four."

The woman on the other end of the line went into a long tirade about the boys of the baby sitter she'd just fired and how badly they'd treated her daughter, who was really delicate because she had allergies. Zoe shut the refrigerator and banged her forehead gently against the door of the freezer section, which was covered with the boy's pictures, drawings and awards. *Why me, Lord?* When the woman intimated she was concerned about leaving her precious Katie with three boys, who, everyone knew, were apt to do get into all sorts of trouble, Zoe felt bound to offer a defense.

"Well, I won't deny that my sons are all boy, Mrs. Jeffries," Zoe said when the woman finally wound down, "and they can be mischievous, but they're good boys. I don't think we'd have a problem with them terrorizing your Katie or doing anything terrible to her."

She listened to the other woman a moment, her eyes widening in disbelief. "You want to come out and look things over and meet us? Well, uh, certainly. I'd be happy for you to. In fact, I insist on it. I'd like to meet you and Katie, too." *Remember, Zoe, you go to hell for telling lies.*

"Yes. Tomorrow evening at six? Wonderful." Zoe gave the woman directions to the farm, bade her goodbye and hung up with mixed feelings of relief and dread. This wasn't as easy as she'd imagined, but then things seldom were. The classified ad had been out almost a week now, and so far, there had been no takers for her as a baby-sitter or for the cabin. Most people felt that it would be out of the way to drive their children to her place before getting to work. Of the few who felt it would be wonderful for their child to have wide open spaces to play in, only one had come to actually check things out and she'd never called back. And now Mrs. Jeffries and the no-doubt spoiled-rotten Katie were coming to look her and the boys over. Zoe gave a little groan at the prospect.

She'd had no better luck with renting the cabin.

When she and Celia had gone to check out the deer hunter's hangout that sat midway in the grove of pine and hardwoods that separated her house from her neighbor's, she'd been surprised to find it in remarkably good repair. It was small—a combined living and dining area, two small bedrooms, a shower-only bathroom and a kitchen straight from the seventies. Zoe had scrubbed the olive-green appliances until they gleamed, painted the tiny bathroom a soft yellow and made new tab-top curtains for every window. She'd decided to offer it either furnished or unfurnished. It would make a great place for the right person. Unfortunately, that person had yet to come along.

The screen door crashed against the wall and Danny, her youngest, shot through the aperture before the powerful spring snapped the door shut. "I'm starving!"

"I know you are," Zoe said. "I've been on the phone with a lady who might bring a her daughter out here to stay while she works."

"A girl?" Danny said. "I don't want no girls out here."

"Any," Zoe corrected. "I don't want any girls out here."

"Well, if you don't want them out here, either, why is she coming?"

Zoe couldn't help smiling. Danny had a good point. She decided to change the subject. "What sounds good for supper?"

"Peanut butter."

As the other boys had, Danny was going through a phase where he practically lived on peanut butter and jam sandwiches. Zoe took what comfort she could in the knowledge that the phase had passed, and Chris and Mike seemed no worse for it.

"How about pork chops, mashed potatoes and creamed corn instead?"

Danny paused at the screen door. "Can I mix my corn and potatoes together?"

Usually, Zoe tried to discourage the food mixing, which seemed to encourage more play than eating, but her conversation with Adelle Jeffries had lowered her resistance. "Why not?"

"You don't think it's gross?"

"Not really. In fact, I used to do it myself," she admitted.

"You did?"

Zoe nodded. She thought Danny seemed disappointed as he pushed open the door and went outside. Grossing people out seemed to rank high on his list of desired accomplishments. She had a feeling that she might have spoken out of turn. Katie Jeffries probably would be terrorized...or at least harassed unmercifully by the boys. The door had barely shut behind him, when Chris came in.

"Danny said we were having pork chops for supper."

"That's right," Zoe said. "Will you peel the potatoes, please?"

"How many?"

"Just peel," she said as the phone rang. "I'll tell you when." She turned on the phone. "Hello."

"Zoe Barlow, please."

The voice was deep, masculine, warm and sexier than any voice had a right to be. "This is she."

"My name Max Murdock. I saw your ad in the paper."

"Which one?" Zoe asked. "The one for a baby-sitter or for the cabin I have for rent?"

"The baby-sitting."

"Oh." She hoped her disappointment didn't show. She'd been thinking that if she could rent the cabin, she might not have to take on the added job of baby-sitter.

"Are you keeping any other children right now?"

"Three," she said, telling the truth. She went into the pantry and took a can of cream-style corn from the shelf. "And your child? Is it a girl or boy?"

"A girl," he supplied. "Annabelle."

"What a beautiful, old-fashioned name," Zoe said, taking the can opener from the drawer.

"Thank you. You mentioned you have a spacious house. Where are you located?"

Zoe explained where the farm was and waited for him to say it was too far out. Instead, he said, "You mentioned a dog. It isn't an aggressive breed, is it?"

"It's a Heinz 57, Mr. Murdock, and the only thing he's aggressive about is getting to his food bowl."

"I suppose he's had all his shots."

"Whoa! That's enough!" she cried suddenly, seeing that Chris had almost filled a pan with potatoes.

"I beg your pardon?" the masculine voice said.

"I'm so sorry," Zoe apologized. "I was talking to my son, not you." She didn't offer the stranger any further explanation. "Now what was it you were asking?"

"About the dog."

"Oh. His shots. Yes. He's had them."

"I couldn't help noticing that you didn't list your qualifications," the deep voice on the other end of the line said.

"Qualifications?"

"Qualifications," he said again. "Have you been keeping children in your home long? Have you worked in a day care? Do you have a degree in child psychology?"

Zoe heard the edge in the man's voice. She'd much rather be talking to his wife. She gave a nervous little laugh and said, "A degree in child psychology? No. And I've never worked in a day care."

"I don't mean to sound rude, Mrs. Barlow—it is Mrs. Barlow, I assume?—but what makes you qualified to take care of my daughter?"

Already depressed, already feeling like the most terrible mother on Earth, Zoe wasn't surprised to feel her hackles rising. Good grief! It was Mrs. Jeffries in the guise of a man! Zoe counted to ten. "Yes," she said, striving not to let her irritation show. "It's Mrs. Barlow. I'm a widow. As for my qualifications…would it put your mind at ease to know I've been keeping children in my home for ten years?"

"Really? That's impressive."

Isn't it? And most days I still have my sanity.

The door slammed shut and Danny rushed in screaming as he tried to outrun Mike, who was hot on his heels and talking about ripping off his brother's head when he caught him. Frustration and despair pushed aside her disapproval. This conversation was doomed, so she might as well just end it. Besides, it wasn't in her to mislead anyone.

"I have three children, Mr. Murdock. Three boys," she said, heaviness in her voice. "Make that three ornery boys. As you no doubt heard, they're rowdy, loud and often obnoxious, probably not the kind of people you want your daughter to be around. But they're my boys, and I love them. As for the kind of care I provide, well, I give them three square meals a day—

most days. I bandage their hurts, wipe their tears, listen to their hopes and dreams, break up their fights. Sometimes I'm cranky and short with them. I'm sorry to say I yell at them sometimes. I haven't had any child psychology, and I've been known to spank on occasion, though I try never to do it in anger. When I go to bed at night, I pray I haven't warped them too badly, that some day they'll understand that I did do my best for them—even though it may not have been good enough—and that they'll love me, anyway." She took a deep breath. "As you can see, there's no need wasting any more of your time talking about my qualifications—or lack of them. I truly hope you find someone you feel is acceptable to take care of your daughter. Goodbye."

Chapter Two

She'd hung up on him! Max stared at the receiver in disbelief. What had he said, anyway? Couldn't the woman tell he was just trying to do his best for Annabelle, the same way she said she did for her three boys? His mind replayed the sound of the slamming door and the yelling of children. No wonder she sounded stressed. He got tied in knots if he had to bathe Annabelle. He couldn't imagine Annabelle times three.

I bandage their hurts...I give them three square meal a day—most days...I listen to their dreams...and hope I haven't warped them too badly. They're my boys and I love them.

Zoe Barlow's method of mothering sounded a lot like his mother's, and the Barlow boys sounded like pretty lucky kids. Max realized that he and Zoe Barlow were in sort of the same situation—left with children to raise, alone. It didn't matter much that they'd arrived at this point in life differently.

I bandage their hurts...I listen to their hopes and dreams...

Her voice, a voice that had sounded pleasant and mellow when she'd first answered the phone, had become indignant, frustrated and a little helpless sounding over the course of their conversation. It intrigued him. Max got to his feet and went to throw away his cola can. Maybe he should call her back and apologize for coming across as overzealous in his search to find a sitter for Annabelle. For some reason, he wanted to meet this person—a woman who was doing her best, even though she was afraid it wasn't good enough. That was a feeling he was all too familiar with. Despite the fact that her place sounded like a zoo and that she'd hung up on him, Max's gut told him Zoe Barlow was the woman he'd been looking for, that she was the closest thing to his mom he was likely to find.

Zoe set the phone receiver aside and swiped at the stray tear that trickled down her cheek. What on earth had gotten into her? She was never so rude to people.

"What's wrong, Mom?" Chris asked. "Was that man mean to you?"

"Not really, honey," she said. "I think I'm just tired of answering questions. Thanks for peeling the potatoes. Why don't you go see if you can keep Mikey from killing Danny?" she asked with a smile. "I'll try to hurry dinner along."

"Sure."

Zoe was setting the pot on the stove when the phone

rang again. Uncertain she could take another grilling, she hoped it was Celia.

"Barlow residence."

"Mrs. Barlow, this is Max Murdock." Zoe opened her mouth to say something, but he rushed on. "Please don't hang up. I'd like to explain."

Zoe was too surprised that he'd called back to do anything but listen as the rich, masculine voice attempted an explanation. Despite her frustration and slight discouragement, she found herself wondering if the man was half as good-looking as his voice made him sound.

"I've been trying to find someone to keep Annabelle for several days, now. I don't mind telling you it's been very frustrating. Believe me, I've talked to some real weirdos."

"If this is your idea of an explanation, Mr. Murdock, let me assure you that it leaves a little to be desired," she said, her irritation on the rise once more. Sexy voice be darned!

"No! That's not—I didn't mean to insinuate that you're—"

"A weirdo? I assure you, I'm not," Zoe said in her most prim and proper voice. "I am curious as to what was in my ad to make you think I was."

Zoe heard a deep sigh filter through the phone lines. "I'm not doing too well at explaining, am I?"

"No, Mr. Murdock, you aren't."

She heard him take a deep breath, as if he needed to brace himself for what he was about to say. "It was nothing your ad said that kept me from calling. It was what it didn't say."

"I beg your pardon?"

"All the other sitters gave—" he paused, as if he were considering whether he should continue "—qualifications."

Zoe felt her hackles rising again. In the next breath, she realized she should at least hear what he had to say without interrupting. He *had* taken the time and trouble to call back after she'd hung up on him. Taking offense when he was trying to explain wasn't doing anything to defuse a situation that had the potential to get out of hand again.

"I see. You have a point, Mr. Murdock. I suppose I should change the ad before it runs again, and I'd like to apologize for my outburst. I'm not usually so prickly, but I've talked to some really strange parents the past few days, myself, and my patience had worn pretty thin."

"It sounds as if we've both had some bad experiences," he said. "Can we start over?"

Be nice, Zoe. You need the money.

"Maybe we should."

"Great!" he said. "I was wondering if it would be okay if Annabelle and I drove out to your place tomorrow and have a look around, let you meet her…you know? See if the two of you get along—that sort of thing."

Zoe thought for a moment. Mrs. Jeffries was supposed to come the following afternoon, but if she could see both parents in one day, it would save her having to spread out the meetings. "That would be fine. How does ten in the morning sound?"

"Ten is fine. We'll look forward to it."

Zoe gave him directions to the farm. As he was about to say goodbye, she asked, "What made you call back, Mr. Murdock? I was pretty rude to you."

There was no answer for several seconds. "You weren't really rude. You just sounded as if you'd reached the end of your rope. Since I was feeling the same way, I could relate. And, after you hung up on me, I thought about the things you said. My mom used to yell at me, too, but all it really took to put me in my place was a look. As a matter of fact, that look still strikes fear in me," he confessed.

Zoe heard the smile in his voice but decided to get to the bottom of things. "It doesn't bother you that I've spanked my boys?"

"A few well-timed swats on the rear never hurt anyone," he said with a short laugh. "I'd know."

The sound of his laughter was as warm and sexy as his voice. Zoe's heart jerked into a faster rhythm. Then, realizing that she was responding to a man for the first time since David's death, she forced herself to return to business. "All right, then," she said crisply. "We'll see you and Annabelle tomorrow."

Annabelle's crying roused Max from a deep sleep. He rolled to his side, glanced at the clock and groaned. Six o'clock! Still, he supposed he should be thankful that she'd slept through the night, something that happened more and more often the older she got. She was probably hungry, he thought, swinging his feet to the floor and pulling a pair of shorts on over his briefs. Covering a yawn, he headed down the hallway to the nursery.

She was standing up, clinging to the rail of the crib, her brown eyes drenched with tears that spiked her long eyelashes. When she saw him come through the door, she held out her arms and cried harder.

"I'm coming," Max said. Approaching the crib, he saw that her nose was running. She'd smeared the thick liquid over her cheek and into her dark hair. Lovely. Still, it was better than changing a dirty diaper. Reaching out, he picked up his daughter and brought her to his bare chest. Immediately, Annabelle silenced, locked her arms around his neck and buried her face against his, snotty nose and all.

"Agh, Annabelle!" he said. "That's nasty!"

As if she were in tune to the censure in his voice, she started crying again. Worse, she began to struggle to get out of his arms. Great. In an automatic gesture as old as mother- or fatherhood, he began to bounce her up and down and pat her diaper-clad bottom, making shushing noises.

"Are you hungry?" he asked, bouncing and patting as he headed out the door and down the hall toward the kitchen. How many hours had it been since she'd eaten? He was starving; no doubt she was, too. He knew he should change her, but a wet diaper could wait until she had something to eat.

"Shh. Daddy'll fix you something to eat." But first things first. *Stop the crying.* Balancing her on his hip, he took a sippy cup from the dishwasher and opened the refrigerator. He filled the cup with apple juice and handed it to her. Again, the crying stopped almost immediately. Poor little thing. Not only was she starving, she must be thirsty. He wet a paper towel and wiped his face, then swiped at Annabelle's, cleaning it as best he could with her turning her head this way and that. When it became apparent that she was about to cry again, he gave up. He'd get the rest when he gave her a bath.

His helplessness was one of the things that made him

so frustrated. His means of communication with Annabelle were next to zilch. He was never sure what to do for her when she cried. He just tried one thing and then another until he somehow, miraculously, hit on something that worked. Sometimes nothing worked, and she either got over what was bothering her or cried herself to sleep, which made him feel less than capable as a parent. Thank God the juice was working for now. With a little luck, it would hold her until he got her cereal fixed. Max strapped her into her high chair and slid the tray into place.

Annabelle clutched the cup with her chubby hands, lifted it to her mouth and tipped back her head. "Mmm," she said, slamming the cup down onto the metal tray.

Next to the "da da" she'd spoken the other day, it was the closest thing to a word Max had heard her say, the nearest thing to real communication he'd shared with her. He couldn't help smiling. "Good, is it? Drink it up for Daddy."

"Da da."

"That's right," he said, feeling that strange warmth spread throughout him as it had when she'd smiled at him the other day. "Daddy."

Annabelle picked up her cup, turned it upside down and let the liquid dribble out. He started to stop her, then remembered how fast she could turn on the waterworks and thought better of it. Letting Annabelle smear her hands through the puddling juice, Max set about getting her breakfast, which was easy, considering all he had to do was open up a jar of fruit and a box of cereal. She'd even taken to eating it with no warming—something he'd discovered one day when he was running late getting her to his mom's. As he sat down and began to spoon the pureed fruit into Annabelle's mouth, he wondered what Zoe Barlow was giving her three boys for breakfast. Did they eat cereal, or did she fix them biscuits, bacon and eggs—a real old-fashioned farm-type breakfast? He found himself wondering if she was as staid and starched as she sounded. Not that there was anything wrong with that in a baby-sitter. Far better that than someone wild and crazy. And, he admitted, her voice had a sweetness to it whenever she wasn't giving him what for. Voices had always interested him. It was always intriguing to see how a person and her voice matched up.

"Someone's coming!" Danny's announcement was accompanied by the sound of tennis shoes slapping the front porch.

"Okay!" Zoe called back, glancing at the clock that hung over the kitchen sink. Ten o'clock on the dot. Mr. Max Murdock was right on time. She untied her apron, tossed it to the countertop and then went to greet their guests. Though she couldn't see it for the grove of pine and hardwood trees, she heard a car coming down the lane that led to the house. Pushing through the front screen door, Zoe wiped her sweating palms down the sides of her floral dress and smoothed the willful strands of her auburn hair toward the loose knot clipped atop her head. The vehicle, a new, creamy gold Expedition, passed the last of the trees and came into view. Zoe fought back a rush of envy. She'd love to have an SUV. Her own Grand Am, almost ten years old, wasn't exactly what she needed for hauling around three boys, a dog and various sports paraphernalia. Oh well, maybe some day.

The truck pulled to a stop, and Max Murdock opened the door and got out. From here, he certainly did justice to his sexy voice. In spite of herself, Zoe felt her heart begin to beat a little faster. He was tall and fit, with broad shoulders that stretched across a moss-green, golf-style shirt. Slim hips were encased in khaki slacks. His hair was dark, short, and looked as if it had a bit of curl to it. The slight wave in his hair was the only thing that looked yielding about him. He took a quick look around, as if he were sizing up the place, or looking to see if there might be someone lurking about. Wary, almost. As if he'd been knocked off stride by something unexpected and didn't intend to be caught off guard again. Intrigued, Zoe stepped closer to the railing. The movement must have caught his eye, because he took a step toward her and said, "Mrs. Barlow?"

"Yes," Zoe said, starting down the broad wood steps that led to the brick sidewalk.

"I'm Max Murdock."

She smiled. He didn't. Not at first, anyway. Then, almost as if he sensed it was expected, he did smile. Zoe wished he hadn't. It should be against the law for such a small thing to change any man so drastically. The smile was lethal, which might be why he used it so sparingly. The simple action revealed a beautiful set of teeth, etched deep grooves in his cheeks and brought little laugh lines at the corners of his eyes into play. Zoe's heart did a backflip. Caught off guard, she paused where she was, reminding herself that his effect on her was caused by deprivation. Then she forced herself to take the few final steps to his outstretched hand. Almost reluctantly, she held out her own hand and found it clasped in a warm, firm grip as solid and unyielding as the man who offered it.

"Nice to meet you," Max Murdock said, before releasing his hold on her.

"You, too," she said, urging the corners of her mouth upward again.

He made a quick survey of her from head to toe. Then he looked past her, turning and taking in the view from every direction. While he was distracted, Zoe was taking in him. He was a very masculine, very attractive man, no doubt about it. She found herself wondering what it was that had made him a single parent. A woman would have to be crazy to let a man like him get away.

Looks aren't everything, Zoe. Just because he looks delicious, doesn't mean he has what it takes to make a good partner.

"It's beautiful out here," he said at last, nodding. "You're right. It looks like a great place for kids to grow up."

"We like it."

"How long have you lived here?"

There was an intensity in his eyes that went beyond the casualness of the question. "Not quite three years," she said. "After my husband died, I thought it would be better for the boys if we got out of the city."

"The city? Little Rock?" he asked with a lift of his dark eyebrows.

"Dallas," she said.

He nodded. "Do you mind my asking how he died? "

If she did, it was too late, she thought. "He was a doctor," Zoe said, meeting his gaze with an almost disconcerting directness. "He went to South America and was there two weeks when he got sick with some kind of virus. He never got over it."

His expression softened. "I'm sorry."

"Yeah," Zoe said. "So am I." She gave him a considering look.

"You're wondering why I'm bringing up my daughter alone." It was a statement, not a question. When she nodded, he said, "My story isn't nearly as heartbreaking as yours."

"Divorce?" He nodded, but didn't offer her any details. Zoe understood his reluctance to talk about it, since the breakup of his marriage must be a fairly recent thing. When David first died, it was months before she could talk about him to anyone without bursting into tears. "Did you bring Annabelle, Mr. Murdock?" she asked.

He nodded. "She fell asleep on the way out, but I imagine she woke up the minute the car stopped. I can't believe she isn't screaming her head off."

"Let's get her," Zoe said. "See how she likes it here."

"That's why we came." He turned toward the back passenger door. "Where are your boys?"

"Oh, they're around," Zoe said, a slight smile curving her lips in spite of herself. "They're watching us right now, trying to size up the situation and see what the *girl* is like."

Max Murdock gave her another of those heart-stopping smiles. "They don't much like girls, huh?"

"They haven't reached the age where the female gender holds much interest—thank goodness. A baby girl might be different. We'll see."

She watched as her visitor opened the back car door and unfastened the restraints on the car seat. Then he reached inside and lifted the baby out. About a year old, she had a mop of dark curly hair and olive-hued skin, like her father's. She must have just awakened, because she was rubbing her eyes with her chubby fists.

Max turned with her in his arms. It was clear to Zoe that he wasn't very comfortable. "This is Annabelle."

As if she understood that something was happening, Annabelle lowered her hands and looked at Zoe, a frown drawing her eyebrows together. She was a beautiful baby with a serious expression—one who seemed to know more than her age would suggest. An "old soul" as Zoe's mother would say.

"Hello, Annabelle," Zoe said, giving a little wave. To her surprise, Annabelle waved back. Zoe laughed. "She's beautiful."

"Thank you."

Zoe held out her arms, to see if the baby would come to her. "Come here, sweetie," she cooed. "Come see me."

To her surprise, and clearly to Max Murdock's, the baby leaned forward, her arms outstretched. Zoe took Annabelle from her father and rested their foreheads against each other. "You're a sweetie pie, aren't you?"

Annabelle gurgled something and turned to her father, pointing. "Da da."

"That's right," Zoe said. "That's Daddy. Is he a sweetie pie?" As soon as she'd said it, she wished she hadn't. What if he mistook her for a man-hungry widow just looking for a nice, single dad? Now that she'd seen the baby, Zoe was thinking that keeping Annabelle might not be such a bad thing. The baby liked her, which was a plus. What she didn't need was to feel uncomfortable around Annabelle's attractive father. As it was, she was far too aware of him for her own good.

"I've been called a lot of things by a lot of people, but a sweetie pie isn't one of them," Max Murdock said with a smile that held more than a hint of sarcasm.

Zoe didn't know how to answer that, so she just smiled. Evidently fascinated by her bright hair, Annabelle grabbed a strand that had worked itself loose. She didn't pull, though, content to just touch.

"Is it always so peaceful out here?" Max asked, looking out across the pasture she leased to Celia and Tom, where a cow and her calf chewed contentedly on the lush green grass.

"Until the boys get wound up," Zoe said. "Thank goodness, there are no neighbors to complain when they do."

"Where's the cabin?"

"The cabin?"

"Yeah. I thought you said you had a cabin for rent."

"Oh, yes, I do."

"Do you mind if I take a look at it?" he asked.

"No," Zoe said, trying not to sound as surprised as she was. Wouldn't it be wonderful if he knew someone who wanted to rent the cabin? Then, if he decided to leave Annabelle with her, she might not have to put up with Mrs. Jeffries and the precious Katie. "Of course not. If you'll take Annabelle, I'll go get the key."

She stepped closer, close enough to get a whiff of some woodsy masculine scent, close enough that when she handed him the baby, her hand was caught for a fraction of a second between the warmth of Annabelle's pudgy body and the heat of Max Murdock's chest. The touch lasted only a second, but it was long enough for her to realize how much she'd missed the warmth and hardness of a man's body beneath her palms. The shock of that thought sent her gaze flying up to his.

"Ouch!" She'd forgotten that Annabelle held a fistful of her hair. In an instinctive gesture meant to ease the tension on the hank of hair, he stepped closer and reached out to loosen his daughter's grasp. Zoe reached up simultaneously, her fingers encountering the warmth of his. Without giving it any conscious thought, she looked up at him. For a fraction of a second, she could have sworn she saw her interest mirrored in his dark eyes, but the moment was gone so quickly, she must have imagined it. He lowered his hand.

"Got it?"

She nodded, working Annabelle's fingers free of the errant strand of hair. Free at last, she stepped back and looked at him. An unreadable expression lingered in his eyes. "I'll just go get the key." Her voice sounded breathless, even to her own ears.

"Fine," he said, nodding.

Without another word, Zoe turned and sped up the steps. Inside, she paused and placed the palms of her hands against her hot cheeks. What was the matter with her? So Max Murdock was an attractive man. She'd met dozens of attractive men since David died.

Get a grip, Zoe. This is potential money in the bank. Don't blow this by acting like a sex-starved ninny.

She grabbed the cabin key from the hook near the back door and retraced her steps through the house. When she got to the front screen, she couldn't believe what she saw. All three of the boys were clustered around Max Murdock and Annabelle. Zoe was stunned. Not only had they come out of hiding but from the sound of things, they were all talking at once.

Max Murdock looked overwhelmed as his eyes darted from one boy to the rest. Clearly, he was out of his depth. Annabelle, though, appeared to be in her element. With the strange sense of comprehension babies and young children seem to have, she'd recognized the boys as being on her level. She was waving her arms in excitement and grinning from ear to ear. Well, at least she wasn't scared of them. Not yet, anyway.

"One at a time, boys," she called. "Mr. Murdock can't answer your questions if he can't understand what you're asking."

"You told us a fib, Mom," Danny said in an accusatory tone. "This isn't a girl. It's a baby."

"Of course she's a baby, stupo, but she's still a girl," Chris said before Zoe could answer. Danny responded by sticking out his tongue at his older brother.

"Can she please stay with us?" Mike asked. "She's so cute."

"That's what Mr. Murdock is trying to decide," Zoe explained.

"Max."

She looked up at him in question.

"Since it seems I'm on a first-name basis with Chris, Mike and Danny, it makes sense that the two of us should call each other by our first names, too, don't you think?"

"I suppose so," she said, trying not to read anything into this new development. "I'm Zoe."

"Zoe. That's a pretty name."

"Thank you," she said, hoping he couldn't tell that her heartbeat had racheted up a notch. To cover her confusion, she turned to the boys. "Would you like to walk to the cabin with us?"

"Yeah!" they cried in unison, the word barely out of their mouths before they turned and raced toward the path that disappeared into the woods. Zoe, Max and Annabelle followed at a more sedate pace. Deciding it was time to get down to business, Zoe asked, "Do you mind my asking what happened with your old sitter?"

"Not at all," he said. "My mom has been keeping Annabelle, but my stepdad wants to do some traveling. They deserve it, but it's really put me in a bind."

She stooped down to move a dead limb that partially blocked the path. "What would the hours be?"

"I'm self-employed, so I'm fairly flexible. We're usually at my mom's by eight. Would that be too early for you?"

Zoe cast him a wry look. "Are you kidding? With my crew and a school bus to catch?" She shook her head. "Eight is fine."

They moved deeper into the thicket. Shafts of sunlight pierced the overhanging tree limbs, dappling the shaded path with gold. "You said you're self-employed. What do you do?" Zoe thought he looked a bit self-conscious.

"I used to be a cop," he told her. "But about a year and a half ago, I sold my first novel."

A cop. That would explain his sharp scrutiny of his surroundings when he'd first gotten out of the truck. Cops were trained to look for anything out of the ordinary. "You're a writer?" Zoe asked, impressed.

"Yeah. I guess I am." He seemed surprised by the admission. "I write thrillers."

"Mm. I love a good psychological thriller. Is your book in the stores?"

"It should be." He looked uncomfortable again. "I

have to tell you, the writing can be a problem as far as my having a set time to pick up Annabelle." She looked at him quizzically. "I try to quit at five or five-thirty, but when the work is going really well, I sometimes lose track of time." He gave a slight shrug. "You should let me know if that's going to be a problem."

Zoe thought about that. Was having him pick up Annabelle later than five any reason not to keep her? "I work evenings as a waitress in town, but if you wouldn't mind the girl who keeps the boys watching Annabelle until you got here, we could maybe work something out. Julie is my friend Celia's daughter. She's only seventeen, but she's very mature and responsible for her age. I trust her completely."

Max looked thoughtful. "That might be a plan. I'd be willing to pay you or the other girl extra for the days I'm late," he said, tempting her even more.

"Hurry up!" Mike cried from the covered porch of the cabin. "We've been here forever!"

"At least all of two minutes," Zoe said, with a quick smile at Max.

"At least," he agreed. He shifted Annabelle to his other arm and looked around while Zoe tried to see the place through his eyes. The small log cabin stood in a sizeable clearing to the right of the woodland trail that continued to Celia's place. Three huge oaks shaded it in the summer, and half a dozen dogwood trees dotted the surrounding area, thriving and blooming beneath the sheltering limbs of the larger trees. Someone had planted a rose bush near the front step, and Zoe knew from years past that it would have a profusion of fragrant pink blooms in another month or so. There were two peony bushes to the left of the steps and a Henrii clematis twined up one of the porch posts and sprawled across the roof. It, too, would bloom soon, creating a drift of white across the cedar shingles.

"It's great," Max said, heading for the steps. He sounded almost…excited?

"Thanks." He and the boys stood aside while she fit the key into the lock and swung the door wide. The boys burst through the aperture and went running through the rooms like a bunch of wild men.

"Boys!" she shouted. "Settle down." The directive didn't make any immediate impression. "I'm sorry they're so rowdy."

"They aren't bothering me," Max said. "My brother and I got pretty loud when we were kids, too." He glanced around the living and dining areas. "I love the pine floors and the rock fireplace."

"So do I." She gestured to her right. "The kitchen is this way." He followed her to the narrow, galley-style cooking area. "I painted the cabinets and walls and put up a border, but there isn't much I can do about the green appliances right now, as ugly as they are."

"The green is fine." He glanced around the room and nodded his head toward the back door. "Is there a porch out back?"

He seemed really interested, she thought. "A small one. And the bathroom is small. There's no tub. Only a shower."

"Hey, Max!" Chris called, rushing into the room.

Zoe pinned him with a glare that stopped him in his tracks. "That's Mr. Murdock to you."

"But he said we could—"

"I don't care—"

"I really don't mind if they call me Max," he said,

cutting off both avenues of argument. "I promise not to think you're a terrible mother if they do."

Zoe nodded and felt a flush creep into her cheeks. "I try so hard to instill respect for older people."

"I realize that," he said. "But I'm not that old, am I?" The last was asked with a wry twist of his lips.

"No." Zoe looked away from the teasing glint in his eyes in hopes her heart would settle down. Pinning Chris with a stern look, she said, "Okay. Since Mr. Murdock doesn't have a problem with you calling him Max, I'll go along with it. But you're to always show him the utmost respect, do you hear?"

"Yes, ma'am." He turned to Max. "Max, is it okay if we take Annabelle out to the front porch swing? We'll be careful."

"Sure." Max leaned over and handed Annabelle to Chris, who plopped her on his left hip like an old pro. "Tell them bye-bye," Chris said in a singsong voice as he waved his hand toward Zoe and Max.

Annabelle looked at him for a moment, then lifted her hand and waved. "Ba-ba."

Chris beamed. "She's really smart, isn't she?"

"I hope so," Max said.

Grinning, Chris disappeared through the house. Bedlam erupted on the front porch, all three of the boys yelling that they all wanted to sit by Annabelle.

"If that doesn't scare her, she's pretty tough," Zoe said.

"She is pretty tough if she's survived eight months alone with me," Max said.

Zoe looked up at him. "It's been hard for you." It was a statement, not a question.

"A little," he admitted. "And you?"

"More than a little."

They stood awkwardly for a moment until Zoe cleared her throat and asked, "Would you like to see the bedrooms now?"

"Yeah, sure."

Max looked the rooms over carefully. "I think there's enough room in the larger bedroom for a computer desk and a filing cabinet, don't you?"

"Computer?"

"Yeah. This place is so quiet, I figure I can double my output."

"You? I assumed you were looking at the cabin for a friend."

"Actually, I was just trying to have a little more time to talk to you and see how Annabelle would react to things. It's pretty clear that she's taken with you and the boys. And I think they like her well enough, even if she is a girl." His smile returned, fleetingly.

Hearing the giggles coming from the front porch, Zoe had to agree.

"Then I started thinking that if I rented the cabin and was late, I wouldn't have nearly so far to go to pick up Annabelle. I wouldn't be so worried about running overtime." He raked a hand through his dark hair. "Am I making any sense?"

"Yes," she said, barely able to contain her excitement. Baby-sitting Annabelle *and* renting the cabin meant that not only could she call Mrs. Jeffries and tell her to go fly a kite, she could give up her night job. Then a sobering thought hit her. She'd be living in very close proximity to Max Murdock, a tantalizing notion but one that she wasn't sure was wise.

A heart-shriveling scream came from the front porch.

"Annabelle!" Zoe and Max cried in unison. They headed for the front door simultaneously. Zoe pushed through the screen first and saw that Chris had Annabelle in his arms, trying his best to silence her. Seeing Max, he handed her over, relieved to be rid of the responsibility.

"Is she okay?" Zoe asked.

"All I see is a big goose egg on her forehead," Max said.

"What happened?" Zoe asked, frantically looking from one wide-eyed boy to the next. Seeing nothing but fear in Mike's and Danny's eyes, she turned to Chris. "Christopher?"

Chris just stood there looking as if he were about to burst into tears. Annabelle's were tapering off some.

"She fell out of the swing and bumped her head," Mike said, his bottom lip trembling. "I just left her for a minute, so I could go get her a flower. I told Danny to swing her."

"I did swing her!" Danny cried.

"Yeah!" Mike yelled at his brother. "Too hard! You have to hold on to her."

"I—"

"Don't blame them. It's my fault."

Zoe and Max turned to Chris. The threatening tears had made good on their attempted escape and rolled down his cheeks. "Mike did go get her a flower, and Danny didn't know he had to hold her so she wouldn't fall out. Mutt had run off, and I went to try to get him to come back on the porch, because Annabelle really likes him."

It was all Zoe could do to stop her own tears.

"She was my responsibility. I told you I'd watch her,

and I didn't. If you think I need a spanking, Mr. Murdock, I understand."

Zoe turned to Max to gauge his reaction.

"I don't think you need a spanking, Chris," Max said with a shake of his head. "I think you've been punished enough."

Chris swiped his fingertips over his eyes. "She won't ever like me again."

"Sure she will," Max consoled. "She'll forget about it."

"I won't forget," Chris said.

"That's good," Max said with an encouraging nod.

"Thanks, Max," Chris said. Max nodded again, and Chris and his brothers left the grown-ups standing on the porch, thankful to have escaped without bodily harm.

Max turned his attention to Annabelle, who had stopped crying and was investigating the pocket of his shirt. He turned to Zoe and held out his hand. "It's a deal, then?"

"What?" she asked, frowning.

"My renting the cabin. You keeping Annabelle for me."

"You still want me to watch her, even though she just got hurt here?"

"You know as well as I do that even when you watch a child like a hawk watching a chicken, they can get hurt. I like it here. Annabelle likes you and the boys. And I was very impressed with the way they all took responsibility for what happened. You've done a good job with them. I think this will be an ideal place for my daughter to stay."

Strangely, the compliment made Zoe feel like crying. She dropped her gaze from his and swallowed. "You haven't even asked how much the rent is or what I charge to baby-sit."

"So tell me," he said seriously, though she thought she saw a hint of a smile in his dark eyes. She quoted what seemed to her a reasonable amount of money for the small cabin and child care. Max stuck out his hand again. "Fair enough."

Grateful, but a bit stunned at the speed by which the whole transaction had taken place, Zoe placed her hand in his. Just that easily, she was a landlady.

Chapter Three

"How did it go?" Celia asked, excitement in her voice. The dust from Max's SUV had barely settled before she burst through Zoe's back door.

"I'll be keeping Annabelle starting next Monday." Zoe's voice held a note of satisfaction.

"Great!" Celia said, sitting down at the table. "How old is she?"

"Eleven months. And she's a doll. She came right to me. Max seemed surprised."

"Max, is it?" Celia asked with a little smirk. "Is he nice?"

"We decided it would be best to be on first-name terms, since I'll be watching his baby. And yes, he seems nice, though a bit standoffish." Zoe paused. "He doesn't smile much."

"What's the rest of his name and what does he do?"

"Max Murdock, and he's a former Little Rock policeman turned thriller writer."

Celia's mouth fell open in disbelief. "A writer? Is he published?"

"As a matter of fact, he is. He's working on his second book."

"Interesting," Celia said. "So he could have some money." She cocked her head to the side and frowned thoughtfully. "Is he good-looking? Old?"

Knowing her friend wouldn't give up until she wrung every bit of information from her, Zoe cast a smile over her shoulder. "I know what you're thinking, but he isn't nearly old enough to have one foot in the grave, even if he does have money, and yes, I believe you could say he's better than average-looking."

"Zoe!"

Zoe was still trying to figure out her attraction to Max Murdock. She'd met men more handsome. Why was it that this particular one made her heart race? "All right, all right! He's very attractive. Not what I'd call classically handsome, but he has that 'it'—you know?"

"You liked him!" Celia said, in an awestruck voice.

"Well, of course I liked him. Otherwise, I wouldn't have agreed to keep Annabelle," Zoe answered with mock exasperation.

"No," Celia said, pointing an accusatory finger at Zoe, "I mean you really *like* him."

"Celia!"

"Don't Celia me. You think he's hot, and I say it's about darn time. I was beginning to wonder if ice water ran in your veins, you seemed so disinterested in men."

"Excuse me," Zoe said, "but you're jumping to conclusions, and don't forget that I've been a little busy keeping a roof over our heads and clothes on our backs. Men haven't been high on my list of priorities. Still aren't. Besides, there is a man in my life, if you count Jack."

"I don't."

Zoe didn't, either. Not really. Jack was the assistant principal at Chris's school, and he'd recently divorced. For some reason, he'd taken to telling Zoe his troubles. She guessed he didn't think she had enough of her own. She held up an empty glass. "Would you like some lemonade and cookies?"

"Sure," Celia said with a slight shrug. "I still think this is a good thing."

"I'm not so sure." Zoe went to the ice maker and filled the glass. "I want this to be a long-term relationship. No!" She pinned her friend with a daunting look. "Don't you dare make any comments about my choice of words." She grew serious. "I mean it, Celia. I may think he's handsome, but don't forget that I don't come into contact with many handsome men. My reaction is normal, but finding him attractive is as far as it's going to go. I don't need anything happening to mess things up."

Seeing her genuine distress, Celia dropped the teasing. "It shouldn't be a problem. You won't be seeing that much of him. Drop off Annabelle. Pick up Annabelle."

Zoe set the glass of lemonade and a platter of cookies on the table. "There will be a tad more interaction than that." Seeing the question in Celia's eyes, she said, "He's renting the cabin. I already got a deposit and a month's rent."

Celia's eyes widened. The hand carrying the cookie to her mouth paused in midair. "You're kidding."

"Nope."

"Wonderful! Maybe you can quit the fish place," Celia said, taking a bite of a chocolate chip cookie.

"I plan to. Maybe Julie could get that job."

Celia washed down the cookie with a swallow of lemonade. "That would be good. My darling daughter is always looking for ways to add to her travel slash college fund. Do we know what happened to Mrs. Max?"

Zoe shook her head. "All he said was that she left. No details. Obviously, it's been since Annabelle was born, so the hurt is pretty recent."

"No kidding. That must have been tough. And it must have been hard on him to suddenly have sole responsibility for a child."

"That's hard on anyone, Celia. Man or woman." Zoe poured some more lemonade into her own glass, took a sip and stared at some phantom place across the room. "I can tell by the way he holds Annabelle that he isn't comfortable with his new responsibility. In fact, I'd say he's scared to death of her, and she knows it."

"He's probably never been around babies. He'll get the hang of it."

"He doesn't seem like the type who wants to." Zoe sighed. "You know, Celia, some people just aren't cut out to be parents." She glanced over at her friend. "Don't get me wrong. It's obvious he wants the best for Annabelle, but I'm not sure he's willing to invest much of himself."

Celia gave a slight shrug. "Maybe being a cop made him that way."

"Maybe," Zoe said with a nod. "And maybe that's what went wrong with the marriage."

* * *

"So what was the baby-sitter like?" Max's mother asked him later that evening as he was having dinner with her and Paul.

"She seemed nice enough." Truth was, Max had thought of little but Zoe Barlow since he left her place. He didn't miss the look that passed between his mother and stepdad.

"Pretty?" Paul asked.

Max frowned. Was Zoe pretty? No. Not really. Pretty was too bland. Beautiful didn't fit, either. She was more striking than pretty. She had a classic beauty, the kind that was often overlooked or mistaken for plainness because it held elements that went far beyond merely pretty. He couldn't deny that she'd made an indelible impression on him.

"She's a redhead," he offered, instead of answering his stepfather's question.

"A redhead, hmm? Sexy?" This was asked with a wiggle of Paul's eyebrows.

"Paul!" Donna chided. "Stop teasing."

"Honey," Paul said. "He's divorced, not dead."

The lighthearted banter passed right over Max as he conjured up an image of Zoe in her modest sundress and the loose cascade of auburn hair twisted atop her head. He saw again the spattering of freckles across the bridge of her nose and over her shoulders. Recalled the scent of roses that had wafted from her body when he'd leaned close to free her hair from Annabelle's grasp. Sexy, no. Wholesome was more like it. Ruthlessly, he pushed away the memory of how his heart had taken a leap when her hand had been imprisoned between his chest and Annabelle's body. The brief contact had been enough to remind him that he'd been celibate for more months than he'd like to think. Any woman could turn him on with a touch. As soon as he thought that, he knew it wasn't true. More than a few women had made a play for him since Cara left, but until today, not one of them had sparked even the smallest bit of interest.

Neither does Zoe Barlow. His mind tried to tell his body something contrary to what he knew in his heart. But just because he felt an unexpected surge of desire didn't mean she held any special interest for him. It was too soon after the divorce. He wasn't ready for a relationship, not even a casual relationship, and something told him that Zoe Barlow would never consent to something casual, even if he were interested. No, she wasn't a one-night-stand type. She was the wedding-ring, do-it-up-proper kind of woman. The thought of remarrying held no appeal and he feared it might never again.

"She's a June Cleaver type," he told Paul finally. "Very motherly and nurturing."

"Sounds perfect for Annabelle."

"I thought so." Max took a swallow of his tea.

"Does she have children?" Donna asked.

"Three little hellion boys."

Paul laughed. "I don't envy her."

"Me, either." Max cast a resolute look at his parents. "I may as well tell you I'm moving out there."

"That was fast," Paul said, never missing a beat.

Max's mouth twisted into a wry smile. "Always a wisecrack," he said. "She had a cabin for rent, and I thought if I moved out there it would solve a lot of the problems that come up when I'm really into the book and can't pick up Annabelle on time."

"Are you sure that's the smart thing to do?" Donna

asked. "You've barely gotten settled in here, and now you want to uproot you both again?"

"It makes a crazy sort of sense to me, Mom, and it's really peaceful out there. I should be able to get a lot of work done."

"What did you think of the boys?"

Max shrugged again. "They were cute kids, and from what I could see, very well brought up. They reminded me of me and Ryan when we were kids."

Paul rubbed his palms together in anticipation. "I can't wait to get a look at this paragon of motherhood. So when do your mother and I get to meet her?"

"Whenever you agree to help me move the big pieces of furniture," Max told him.

Paul pasted an aggrieved expression on his face. "I believe that's blackmail."

"Think of it as doing unto others as you'd like them to do unto you."

"I'm still not so sure about this move," Donna said.

"I don't plan to live there forever, Mom. Just until I can get this book behind me and sort of get on a little better footing with Annabelle."

"I hate to point out what's so obvious, honey, but you're never going to get better with her if you don't spend more time with her," his mother said.

Max's jaw tightened in irritation. "I'm doing the best I can, Mom. I'm not like Paul. I don't have that father gene he was born with."

The expression on Paul's face turned grave. "Then you'd better work at developing it, Max. You have to be a part of her life, and I don't mean just feeding her and changing her diapers. You have to love her."

Max surged to his feet. "I do love her," he said, his

voice a low growl of indignation, knowing as he said it
it was truer than he would have ever believed. "I just
can't relate to her. I can't get used to all the things she
does, what she expects."

Donna reached out and took his hand. "If you love
her and you keep trying, it will come, son. I promise."

It had been quite an eventful day, Zoe thought as she
checked the sleeping boys before heading for bed herself. After Celia left, she'd called Mrs. Jeffries and can-
celed their appointment, telling the fussy woman she'd
filled all her spots. Adelle Jeffries didn't sound too
thrilled but was fairly decent about it. Max had called
just after dinnertime, asking questions he'd forgotten to
ask—about proper wiring for his computer, laundry arrangements and whether he could begin moving things
the following day while his mother was around to help
with Annabelle. Zoe had assured him it would be fine,
but when they'd hung up, she'd stared at the phone for
long, contemplative moments, asking herself again if
she'd gotten herself into something she'd later wish
she hadn't.

It was true that they were both single, but that didn't
mean Max was unattached. She'd had time to get over
the pain that invaded her life when David died. After
three years, any tears she might cry were more tears of
regret and nostalgia. The pain of losing him had lost its
sharp edge; it was more of a throbbing ache that came
to her when she least expected it. When she was tired.
Lonely. Worried. That's when the memories and the
self-pity assaulted her with all their sweet agony. That's
when she missed him the most.

There were times, though, mostly happy times, times

when one of the boys would say something that sounded like something David might say. Times when Chris stuck out his tongue in concentration while he was doing his homework, or Mike put his hands on his hips and stood just so. Times Danny teased her and she would think of David and wish he were there to see how their boys were growing up. Times she wished he could share in the pride she felt at their accomplishments, mourn with her over the things they did wrong, agonize with her over whether she was doing all she could to bring them up right.

Max Murdock was different. His divorce and his pain were fresher. He hadn't had time to work through the anger he must feel over his ex-wife's leaving, let alone enough time to deal with the pain. He was divorced and while his ex might not be in his life, she and whatever had happened were still in his thoughts. Zoe suspected it would take more than a few months for him to rid himself of the pain of it. She sensed that he had about all on his plate he could handle and suspected that the last thing he wanted or needed was some woman going gaga over him.

She sighed and went into the bedroom, taking her nightgown from the drawer and heading toward the shower. The water was hot, and she let it beat down on her head and body, washing away the day's weariness and a nagging sense of restlessness. She washed her hair and scrubbed at her body with an oatmeal soap that left her feeling refreshed and invigorated, at least on the outside.

As she was drying off, she caught a glimpse of herself in the steam-clouded mirror, something that happened almost every time she got out of the shower. This time, though, she wasn't hurrying to get ready to go somewhere, wasn't ready to fall into bed, wasn't being yelled at to fulfill one of the boy's wishes. Catching the eye of the woman in the mirror, she paused, the towel against her cheek. Her long auburn hair was plastered to her head and clinging to her freckle-dusted shoulders. Did she look older than her thirty-two years? She'd been so preoccupied with keeping things together since David died that she hadn't had much time to spend on herself, much less the inclination. Had she let herself go? She'd never considered herself to be a beauty, but she knew she wasn't ugly, either. She'd always thought that she looked pretty average. She lowered the towel, stepped closer to the vanity and narrowed her eyes in self-examination. There were just the beginnings of tiny crow's feet at the corners of her eyes, and a few lines in her forehead. She'd always had good skin and that hadn't changed. She walked three or four evenings a week and had maintained her weight fairly well—even having three babies—and was within six or seven pounds of her high school weight. She turned and looked at her derriere over her shoulder. While it might not be as firm as it once was, it wasn't bad. Her waist was still small, and her breasts were far from sagging, probably because they were small, too. With a sigh, she tossed the towel in her hand at the image in the mirror and pulled her cotton gown over her still dripping head. Then she picked up the towel and wrapped it around her wet hair, turban-style.

Why was she suddenly so interested in her looks? Was it because Max Murdock was the first man in eons to jolt her into an awareness of her femininity with his soft, slow, sexy but somewhat rusty smile? Or was it because she was finally emerging from the cocoon of grief she'd lived in so long and was preparing to get on with her life? A part of her felt sad at leaving David behind, but another part of her felt a glimmer of excitement.

Ah, David, I do miss you and what we had.

And she did. But it was time to move on. Her unexpected response to Max Murdock made it official. Somehow, at some time, she had passed a turning point. She was ready to get on with her life, ready for a chance to love again. And maybe, more important, she was willing to take the chance that somewhere out there, there was a man who would love her and her boys and want to be the husband and father her family needed. David would be a hard act to follow, and it might be difficult to find a man who would want to take on her boys, but as Celia had reminded her, women with children married successfully every day. She'd just have to be prepared for the possibility that heartache, not happiness, might lay somewhere in the road ahead.

Feeling both sad and hopeful, she went back into Chris's room. Clad only in his underwear, he lay on his back, one arm flung over his head, the other lying across his stomach. David's favorite sleeping position. Zoe felt a little smile of regret on her lips. Chris was getting so tall. In three years, he would be a teenager. Her heart ached for the journey she knew lay ahead of him. She pressed a kiss to his forehead and smoothed the hair, so like his father's, away from his forehead with loving tenderness.

Then, she went into the room Mike and Danny shared. Danny lay on his stomach, Mike on his side. An incredible feeling of inadequacy filled her. Tears sprang into her eyes. They were so precious, so special. They came into the world so innocent and pure. However they turned out, it would be her doing. A scary, sobering thought. She was doing her best, but was it ever enough?

After gazing her fill at the sleeping boys, she tiptoed from their bedside and went to her own room. Things were changing, and she hoped she was ready for the next round of what life had to offer her.

The next morning, Max took Annabelle to his mother's, who was ready with an apology. "If you want to move out there, it's none of my business," she said. "I need to learn to keep my mouth shut."

"You might need to, but it'll never happen," he said, kissing her cheek. "And you wouldn't be you if you did."

Donna gave a reluctant smile. "Paul asked you what Zoe looks like, but what is she really like? And yes, I know I'm being nosy, but I'm...interested."

"She's like you," Max said, smiling at her choice of words. "She reminds me of you trying to bring up Ryan and me." He explained about Annabelle falling out of the swing and how each of the older boys had taken their share of the blame. "It gave me a good feeling to think that Annabelle would have that kind of teaching."

"She sounds very nice," his mother said. "She might be good for you and Annabelle...in a lot of ways."

Max shot her a withering look. "Forget it, Mom. I'm not interested in forming a relationship with any woman right now."

"I didn't mean to imply that there should be anything

between the two of you. It's just natural for that possibility to cross your mind when two people are available."

"Well, it isn't a possibility as far as I'm concerned. I have absolutely zero interest in anything but finishing this book."

"All right. I respect that, but please don't let what Cara did to you spoil the rest of your life."

"What do you mean?" Max asked, his eyebrows drawing together in a frown.

"Being a cop made you a little suspicious of the rest of the world, kept you from getting too close to people. Since Cara left, you've gotten even worse at keeping people at arm's length, and to my way of thinking, you spend too much time alone."

"Whoa!" he said, holding up a silencing hand. "Let's not forget that the work I do now demands that I spend time alone."

"I know that," Donna said with a gentle smile. "But what about when you quit for the day? When was the last time you went to a movie or out to eat? Or on a date?"

Max raked his mind for an answer. "I have to take care of Annabelle in the evenings, which doesn't leave much time for nightlife. But even if I had the time, I sure as heck don't have any desire to get caught up in the dating game just yet."

"I understand that, but you know that Paul and I worry about you, Max. I understand that what's happened will take some time to get over, but I'm afraid it's going to leave you a bitter man. Don't let that happen. Please."

It wasn't often his mother begged for anything, even

less often that he saw tears in her eyes. He saw them both now, and for the life of him, he didn't know what to say to ease her fears. He knew everything she said was true, but he'd had no real desire to change things. Somehow, it suited him to be at home alone with Annabelle. He hoped that sometime in the future that would change, but for now, he had no desire to pursue the things that made other people happy.

Happy. He wasn't sure he would ever be fully happy again. He certainly hadn't felt that way in his marriage and he really didn't feel that way now. Contentment was a different matter. He felt content to put in his hours in front of the computer and spend his nights in front of the television, his mind focused on some inane sitcom or mediocre drama. There was no chance for any surprises in his life, and he liked it that way. Between the foul-up when he'd been shot on the job and Cara's leaving, he'd had about all the surprises he could handle in one lifetime.

"Cara wasn't right for you, Max," his mother said when he didn't respond to her earlier statement. "She was a nice enough girl, but Paul and I knew from the first that she wasn't for you."

Max couldn't hide his surprise. His mother and stepdad had always seemed to get along with Cara. "I thought you liked her. Why didn't you say something?"

"We did like her, and what could we say?" Donna countered. "You were a grown man, and you seemed so much in love."

"We were. In the beginning. But she couldn't take the job."

"Being married to a policeman is hard," Donna agreed. "There were times I was so worried about your father that I hardly slept for days on end. But his heart got him in the end, not the job, and that taught me a valuable lesson."

"What's that?"

"Don't borrow trouble. Don't second-guess your decisions. We can't change the things we've done, good or bad. All we can do is try to be a better person in the future than we were in the past. And above all else, cherish every moment of your life."

She paused. When Max didn't respond again, she gave a self-conscious laugh. "Sorry. I didn't mean to preach."

"You weren't preaching," he said with an affectionate smile. "You were just giving me one of those mom lectures." He moved closer and gave her a hug. "Don't worry about me, Mom. I know I've been a mess the past few months, but I just need some time to regain my equilibrium."

She reached up and cradled his face between her palms. The tears were back in her eyes. "I only want the best for you, Max. I just want you to be happy."

When Max left his mother's, he spent the rest of the morning at the computer, though his mind never strayed too far from the things she'd told him. It was hard to act happy-go-lucky when his world had been turned inside out. When he was on the force, things had been simple. Black and white. Good and bad. Right and wrong. Now home was work, but his place didn't really feel like home anymore. It didn't feel like work, either, for that matter. It was just a place. Before Cara left, he'd often felt alone, even when she was in the house. Now he *was* alone, except for Annabelle, but it wasn't that same empty feeling he'd experienced when he and Cara were together. And there was Annabelle. Nothing was black and white with her. She was an unknown, something he hadn't been able to come to terms with, a constant reminder of Cara, whom he'd once loved. He wasn't sure of anything when it came to his daughter— what was right or wrong—least of all how to deal with her emotional needs. He couldn't even deal with his own, so how could he be expected to deal with hers, especially when he had no clue to what they were?

Frustrated by his inability to get the words on the page, he went to a nearby liquor store to get some empty boxes to start packing. That shouldn't take much mental power. He filled several boxes, loaded them into the Expedition's back and the rear seats, and drove out to his new home.

As he drove, he felt a twinge of excitement. Though small, the cabin was the perfect place to create. He'd felt it from the moment he'd seen it sitting in the middle of the clearing. Though it wasn't exactly isolated, it was away from the noise of town. He could hear birds instead of sirens and smell the fecund scent of the earth instead of gasoline fumes. And though it sat between Zoe's and her neighbor Celia's houses, neither of them could be seen for the trees, giving him the feeling of being shut off from the world. He would have no interruptions. And, when he finished for the day, he wouldn't have to get in the car and drive across town to pick up Annabelle. It was a perfect situation. He was lucky to have found it.

Chapter Four

Max pulled into the drive, passed the rear of Zoe's house and drove through the narrow lane that meandered through the trees to the cabin. As it had the day before, seeing the cabin nestled in the clearing gave him a feeling of having come home, which was ridiculous, since he'd been born and raised in subdivisions. He pulled as close as possible to the back porch and, tucking a box under his arm, unlocked the door. Zoe must have been there earlier, because the windows were open. A light spring breeze carried the scent of something sweet and fresh into the room. The living and dining areas were still empty, but a vase of fresh-cut garden flowers, most of which he couldn't identify, sat on the mantle—a feminine touch to welcome him to his new home. He opened the front door, giving the fresh air another avenue in, and carried the box to his bedroom. He was on his fourth box when he heard Zoe calling his name.

"In the kitchen!" he called back. He heard her footsteps on the wood floor and, in a matter of seconds, she appeared in the doorway. Her hair was pulled back into a jaunty ponytail and she was wearing a teal-green and white-striped scoop-neck cotton shirt and a pair of matching green shorts. Whether or not he was interested in her as anything more than a baby-sitter for Annabelle, Max couldn't help noticing that she had a nice shape and great legs. He felt his groin tighten in typical male appreciation, which only made him feel more than a little bit irritated. He consoled himself with the notion that admiring an attractive woman's attributes was just a male thing.

"Hi," she said, smiling at him.

He set the two glasses he was holding inside the cabinet. "Hi."

She held up an insulated bag. "I brought you some cold soft drinks in case you get thirsty while you're unloading your things."

Max forced his irritation aside. How could he be angry with her for something that was his problem? He reached for the proffered bag and set it on the countertop. "Thanks. I appreciate your opening the windows, too."

She wrinkled her nose. "It smelled musty, even though I was just in here cleaning a week ago." She glanced through the door to the dining area. "I'm sorry the furniture I offered you isn't here yet, but my friend's husband had plans yesterday evening. It's still at my house."

Max unzipped the thermal bag, pulled out a soda and

popped the top. "No problem. My stepfather is going to help me move some of my big pieces this evening. We'll come get them then."

"Great. I'll have everything ready to go." She looked around and pointed to the box. "Do you want me to put your kitchen things away while you carry in the other boxes?" When he hesitated, she added, "I have an hour before the boys get home. Until then, I'm all yours."

Now there was something to think about, Max thought, his gaze unaccountably roaming the length of her bare legs. The smile on her face vanished, replaced by a stricken look, as if she realized that her choice of words held a double meaning. "If you don't like where I put things, you can always move them later."

"Right." Like Zoe, Max thought it politic not to make anything of the double entendre. He took a long swig from the soda can and set it on the counter. "I'll bring in some more boxes."

He turned and went back outside, thinking about what had just happened. He'd been around the block a time or two and had been considered something of a ladies' man before he'd gotten married. He'd seen it all and heard it all, so in the second after Zoe had told him she was all his for an hour, he'd thought she was making a play for him. But the expression on her face as soon as the words left her mouth told him otherwise. It had been nothing more than a slip of the tongue. Zoe Barlow wasn't the kind of woman to make a bold play for a man. She was the kind of woman who worked her way into a man's life and his mind until she got a good grip on his heart. That kind was far more dangerous.

A sudden thought hit him. Was that why she'd offered to help him, why she'd brought the soda, opened up the house and picked him the bouquet of flowers on his mantel? With a determined effort, he pushed the troubling thoughts from his mind and carried another box into the house. For almost an hour, he and Zoe worked side by side, putting away the contents of the boxes, talking only when she asked where she should put something. When all the boxes that could be emptied had been, Max thanked her for her help.

"I needed an afternoon project," she said, swiping her hands down the sides of her shorts.

"You're the first landlord—excuse me, landlady—who's ever helped me get settled in."

"Have I committed a terrible faux pas?" she asked. "I've never been a landlady before. All I know is that any time I've moved, I've needed every bit of help I could get. And it's nice to share some company with someone who's over ten." As if on cue, the sound of little boys' voices filtered in through the open door.

"Oh, no!" Zoe said, looking at her own watch. "I'd intended to be back at the house before they got off the bus."

"It's okay," Max said. "We're finished."

The sound of the boys' shoes pounding up the wood steps and across the porch announced their arrival. To their credit, they did stop at the front door, tempering their enthusiasm long enough to knock.

"Mom!" Chris called, putting his hands on either side of his eyes and peering through the mesh into the room. The other two boys did the same. "Are you in there?"

"Yes, I'm here," Zoe called. "Don't come in. I'm heading home."

"Aw, man! We wanted to see Max," Mike said, disappointment dripping from his voice.

Max wouldn't have been human if he hadn't admitted to feeling a bit pleased. "Come on in," he said. The door opened and the boys burst into the room, braking to a halt just feet from where the adults stood. Max noticed that Mike's and Danny's hair, the same color as their mother's, was mussed and sweaty. Chris still looked as fresh as he'd no doubt looked when he got on the bus that morning.

"Hi, Max!" the trio said, almost in unison.

Smiling at the genuine happiness in their eyes but a little uncomfortable with their unabashed hero worship, Max shoved the tips of his fingers into the front pockets of his jeans. "Hi. Did you guys have a good day at school?"

"School stinks," Danny said. "I'd rather stay home with Mom."

"He's in preschool," Zoe said. "Cutting the apron strings has been pretty hard for him."

"I don't remember us cutting any strings off your aprons," Danny said.

"It's a figure of speech," Zoe explained. "It means that you've had a hard time not being with me all day."

"Oh," Danny said. "Yeah." He looked at Max with a hint of sorrow in his eyes. "I guess Annabelle will take my place now, huh?"

Anxiety assailed Max. Were they going to have the equivalent of sibling rivalry here? He hoped not. What could he say to ease Danny's apprehension? He searched his mind and finally settled for an explanation he thought sounded like something his mother might say. "No one could ever take your place, Danny. Annabelle will make her own place."

Danny turned to Zoe. "Is that true, Mom?"

"Of course it is. Annabelle will keep me company while you're at school. And once she really gets to know you all, she'll be just as glad to see you when you come home as I am."

"Do you think so?" Mike ask, his eyes wide with excitement.

Zoe's smile was gentle. "I know so. There's something else I bet you haven't thought of."

"What?" Danny asked.

"You can teach Annabelle some of the things you learn at school. She won't be able to learn everything, but she'll love you teaching her things like colors and shapes and hearing you sing the songs you know."

"I get to be the teacher?" Danny said, beaming. "Cool."

Max thought Zoe's attempt to make Danny's schooling an integral part of his interaction with Annabelle was a stroke of genius. Some people really did have that parenting gene.

"Is her head okay?" Chris asked, breaking into Max's thoughts.

Once again, Max found himself impressed. Not many ten-year olds would think to ask about another child's welfare. "It's fine. Thanks for asking."

"Where is Annabelle?" Mike asked.

"With her grandma."

"We don't have a grandma," Danny said sadly.

"Daniel Barlow!" Zoe said. "You most certainly do have a grandmother. Two, in fact, as well as two grandfathers."

"Well, they don't live here, and we hardly ever get to see them, so it's the same thing as not having any," he said, jutting out his chin.

Zoe sighed. "You may be right, sweetheart, but it can't be helped." She turned to Max. "My parents live in Florida, and David's live in Houston. We see them as often as we can, but evidently, it isn't often enough."

"I'm not sure any kid can ever get enough of Grandma," Max said in all seriousness.

"Good point." Zoe held her arms wide, ushering the boys toward the front door. "Come on. Let's go find you a snack. Max has to go get another load." There was the general sound of dissent, but they went without any fuss.

They were at the doorway when Max called her name.

She turned, a questioning look on her face.

"Thanks for the soda."

"You're welcome. See you later."

Max nodded and watched them leave, satisfied that Zoe Barlow was no femme fatale just a gracious lady. And thinking that her tush was as definitely as nicely shaped as her legs....

It was almost six when Zoe heard the sound of an approaching vehicle. She glanced out the window and saw both a red truck and Max's Expedition coming down the lane. From the looks of things, both vehicles were loaded. It would probably be a while before they got everything unpacked and came to get the furniture she was letting Max use. Maybe Max and his stepfather would want to take a break and have a piece of the cake she'd just taken from the oven and something to drink.

The sudden thought that she might be going over-board on this hospitality thing gave her pause. Would

Max think she was interested in him? She didn't want to give him the impression she was after him. Maybe she should ease off.

She was smearing icing on the bottom layer several minutes later, when Chris, fresh from his bath, came into the kitchen and hoisted himself to the cabinet top to watch. "Can we have some cake before we go to bed?"

She flashed him a smile. "Sure. Why not? You're a growing boy, aren't you?" He didn't answer, and as she placed the second layer of cake on the first, she asked, "Is something bothering you, Chris?"

"I was just wondering what happened to Annabelle's mother. Did she die?"

Zoe was always amazed at how much deeper her children's thoughts were than what she expected them to be. She was also amazed at how hard it was to answer some of their questions. "She isn't dead. At least, I don't think she is. Max said something yesterday about her leaving."

Chris's eyes held blatant disbelief. "Leaving? You mean she just left one day and didn't come home?"

"I don't know, Chris," she told him honestly. "He didn't say, and I didn't want to pry."

"Why would she do that?" he asked. "How could she leave Annabelle? She's so cute. And Max…how could she leave him? He's really nice."

Like Chris, she had been asking herself these same questions ever since Max left the day before. "I can't answer that for you, and yes, Max does seem nice, but sometimes things with grown-ups are more complicated than they are to kids. Sometimes things happen and we're forced into doing things we might not do otherwise."

Chris thought about that for a moment and nodded. "Like you had to start baby-sitting and rent the cabin because you need more money to help pay the bills since Dad isn't here."

"Right," Zoe said around the lump in her throat. Chris was too young to have to bear the burden of their limited finances.

"Don't cry, Mom."

"What makes you think I'm going to cry?" she asked, forcing a smile for him.

"Your voice is all funny and your eyes are all shiny."

"You're so smart," she said gruffly, ruffling his hair. Determined *not* to cry, she scooped up another spatula of frosting.

"It's going to be okay, Mom," Chris said. "Max is here now."

Zoe's heart gave a painful lurch. Was renting the cabin to a single man the right thing to do? Would the boys react to any man the way they had to Max? Was she setting them up for a fall? *Do you have a choice?* Max was the only one who had come along and wanted the place, and she really did need the money.

Before she could answer those questions, Mike came running into the room—Danny right behind him—grinning and yelling, "Max is here!" Smiling, Chris jumped down from the cabinet top.

"Well, go and let him in while I finish icing the cake," Zoe said brightly, fighting the threat of tears again. It was heartbreaking that a virtual stranger could evoke such joy in them. She knew they missed David, especially Chris and Mike, who truly remembered him. But she'd never known just how starved they were for a man in their lives until now. Until Max stepped out of his SUV a few days ago, she'd had no idea how starved *she* was for a man's attention. Zoe felt another sudden rush of apprehension and wondered again if she'd done the right thing. Would he be all the boys thought he was? Could he fill the void in their lives? And more important, was it fair for them to expect him to?

Max got out of Paul's truck as the front door burst open and all three of Zoe's boys rushed through, wide smiles on their faces, calling his name. While it pleased him that they'd taken a liking to him, Max wasn't used to such unfettered enthusiasm. As with Annabelle, he wasn't sure just what to do, how to react. He risked a look at his stepfather, who was watching, a contemplative expression on his face.

"Come on in," Chris said. "Mom's putting icing on a cake." He turned to Paul and held out his hand, which he took after a moment of surprised hesitation. "Hi. I'm Chris Barlow. These are my brothers, Mike and Danny."

"Paul Fielding," he said, pumping the boy's hand. "Max's dad."

"Come on in. Mom's got the furniture all ready to move."

The five went to the front door single file—Max leading, the boys following close on his heels and Paul bringing up the rear. Zoe stood at the open door, a welcoming smile on her face. Max's initial thought was that it was nice to be greeted at the door, something that had never happened in all the years he and Cara had been together. His second thought was that she looked sad for some reason. The thought brought an inexplicable ache to his heart.

"Hi," she said, with a slight smile. "Come in."

Max and Paul stepped inside and after Max made the introductions, Zoe asked, "Did you get everything?"

"I think we'll have one more load for the truck and a couple more loads for the SUV. I think it's all going to fit okay, though."

"Good," she said. "Come on back, and I'll show you where the furniture is."

"Mom," Mike said, "Can we have some cake and milk?"

"Yes, but let Chris cut it for you."

"Yes, ma'am."

While the boys ran to the kitchen, Max and Paul followed Zoe to a spare bedroom that was being used for storage. "Here's the sofa and chair," she said, indicating an almost-new green, tan and navy plaid sofa and matching chair. "The previous owner of the house had to go to a nursing home, and his family sold the furniture with the house." She smiled. "They didn't want the 'junk.'"

"It's very nice junk," Paul said, looking around the room.

"That's what I thought. I don't need it, though. I'm letting the boys finish off my old sofa." She shrugged and rubbed her hand over the upholstery in a soft caress.

For a fleeting instant as their eyes met, Max imagined it was his flesh her hand was skimming over so lightly. An acute awareness of her swept over him. He had to force his mind back to what she was saying.

"This one looks masculine, and I thought the plaid would contrast nicely against the log walls." She pointed to a chest of drawers that had been painted a creamy white. "That's the chest I thought would be good in Annabelle's room, and this," she pointed to a headboard and chest on the left side of the room "—is the bed I was talking about for your room."

"Hey, Max!" Danny called from the doorway. "I brought you and Mr. Fielding some cake."

The arrival of her youngest son was a welcome relief. There had been a strange look in Max's eyes a few seconds ago. If she didn't know better, she would have mistaken it for desire. She turned to Danny, who stood in the doorway, a saucer with a slab of chocolate cake on it in each hand. She exhaled a relieved breath. His enthusiasm to play host had saved her from having to make the decision about whether or not to offer cake to Max and Paul.

"Is this okay with you?" Max asked.

"There's plenty of cake."

Max questioned his stepfather with a look.

"I always have time for chocolate cake," Paul said.

"Okay, then." Max crossed the room and took the two small plates from Danny. "Thanks, buddy," Max said. "If it's okay with you, we'll have it in the kitchen."

"Sure!" Danny turned and raced toward the kitchen. "He's staying, Chris! I told you he would."

Zoe offered Max an apologetic smile and started toward the door. "Follow me, and I'll get you some milk to go with that cake."

"Milk sounds good," Max said, falling into step behind her.

"Your boys are really great, Mrs. Barlow," Paul Fielding said as they entered the spacious kitchen. "Their enthusiasm reminds me of Max and his brother Ryan when they were kids."

Zoe smiled and gestured for them to have a seat at the table, where the boys were already attacking their cake. "Sometimes it's more than enthusiasm, but thanks. And please call me Zoe. I'm sure we'll be seeing quite a bit of each other now that Max is moving to the country."

"Can I have more cake, Mom?" Danny asked.

"No, sir. Everyone finish up and go get your teeth brushed. It's almost bedtime." The declaration was met with a chorus of, "Aw, Mom."

"We've got to get with it, too," Max said to Zoe. "Thanks for the cake. It was delicious." To the boys, he said, "Thanks for inviting us. I'll probably see you tomorrow."

"Bye, Max," they said in chorus.

Max and Paul finished their cake, and Zoe told Paul to pull his truck around to the front door.

"I'll do that," Paul said. He held out his hand, which Zoe took. "I enjoyed meeting you and your boys, Zoe, and the cake was delicious."

"Thank you."

Neither she nor Max spoke as Paul went to move the truck.

"I'm sorry about the boys already making a nuisance of themselves," Zoe said.

"Since when does inviting someone for cake constitute being a nuisance? Actually, I've been a little concerned that they're sort of unintentionally pushing me off on you."

"Oh, no! They're not."

Before Zoe could say anything else, she heard the sound of Paul's footsteps on the porch. Zoe led them back to the spare room and watched as they loaded the two chests and the chair. When they moved the mattress, Zoe was surprised to see a canvas between it and the box springs. Suspecting what it was, she went to pick it up, but Max beat her to it.

"What's this?" he asked, turning the picture around and holding it at arm's length.

The answer to his question was obvious. It was an oil painting of a man leaning against the porch railing of another house. A tall man wearing sneakers, jeans and a chambray shirt with sleeves rolled up to the elbows. A man with light brown hair, bluer-than-blue eyes and a teasing smile. She'd painted it a year before he'd left to go to South America.

"Your husband."

Zoe wasn't even aware that she'd been holding her breath until Max spoke, rousing her from her trance. Her breath eased from her in a silent hiss. "Yes."

"Chris looks just like him," Max said. "And Danny has his eyes."

"I think so, too." Zoe heard the breathless quality in her voice and was surprised she could speak at all, she was so taken aback at seeing David's likeness. She had taken it from the wall of the home they'd shared, because she hadn't been able to bear the pain it evoked. When she'd moved, she'd told her mother to put it somewhere it wouldn't get damaged. She hadn't set eyes on it in almost three years.

"You painted this?" he asked, noticing the signature in the right-hand corner of the painting. Paul moved close enough to look over Max's shoulder.

She nodded. "I have a degree from the Art Institute in Dallas."

"It's fantastic," he said.

"Better than that," Paul added.

She felt her face flame at the unexpected praise. In all honesty, she knew it was the best thing she had ever done. "Thank you." She reached out to take the painting. "Here. I'll put it somewhere out of the way."

As the painting was transferred from Max's hands to hers, their gazes met. "With talent like that, why aren't you putting it to use?"

"I do, a little. Or did. I used to sell the occasional painting when we lived in Dallas, but since I moved, I haven't picked up a paintbrush." *Not since David died.*

"Maybe you aren't aware of it," Paul said, "but you're in one of the hottest spots in the country for art. Hot Springs has a fast-growing colony of artists, lots of tourists and more galleries every day. With your talent, you could be making a nice living."

"Paul's right," Max added.

Despite her embarrassment at their seeing the picture, she had to admit their comments roused an inkling of interest in her. She did know that in the past few years, Hot Springs had been making a name for itself as an artist's mecca, but somehow, she'd never thought about it as a place for her, or considered the possibility that her talent might be above average.

"My interest was always in advertising," she said. "I never thought about trying to get into fine art and when the babies started coming, I decided to put it all on hold for a while. I do sell a few pressed-flower and watercolor fairy pictures to a gift shop in town." She didn't tell them that since David died, she'd been too busy grieving, raising children and trying to make ends meet to even consider that painting might eventually become a real moneymaker. Now, two people were telling her it could be. Were they right?

"You're wasting your talent by not trying to pursue this," Max told her, gesturing toward the picture.

Though she knew his heart was in the right place, his choice of words hit her the wrong way. "It's never a waste of time trying to be a good parent, especially if you're the only parent your child has," she said, her voice intense with feeling.

Max looked as if she'd struck him. For a moment she didn't understand, but then she realized that he must have applied the words she'd said in connection with herself to him and his situation. But why would that upset him? From everything she could see, he was doing his best for Annabelle.

"I'm sorry," he said. "Believe me, I never meant my comment as anything but a compliment. You're to be commended for putting your boys first, but in my estimation—which may not be much—I think you have a tremendous talent, and it's a shame for you not to be capitalizing on it." He smiled one of those rare smiles. "Even if your success would mean I'll be looking for a new baby-sitter."

She shook her head and gave a wry twist of her lips. "You don't have to worry about that any time soon. But you and Paul have given me something to think about. Maybe I could start trying to work again at night when the boys are asleep."

Feeling uncomfortable and not knowing exactly why, Zoe drew a deep breath and pasted a smile on her face. "This isn't getting the furniture moved, is it? I'll go clean up the kitchen, and you guys go ahead with whatever you need to do." Without waiting for a response, she turned and left them standing there.

* * *

When Max finally pulled into his driveway that night, he was dead tired. It had taken two trips to move the things from Zoe's to the cabin. When they'd finally finished, he'd called to her, and she'd come to tell them good-night. The awkwardness he'd felt between them when she'd left him and Paul in the spare room had vanished. They'd said their good-nights, and he'd heard the lock click behind him as he and Paul descended the porch steps.

As he drove home, he thought about Zoe's little spurt of indignation. He'd never meant to anger her. All he'd wanted to do was let her know he thought she had a lot of talent, talent she should be sharing with the world in some way. He sighed in frustration. Evidently, his people skills were less than perfect. Maybe it was from having been a cop so long. Police work was an occupation that required a certain amount of secrecy, a certain amount of subterfuge and a certain amount of aggression. Women wanted a man who was truthful, faithful and malleable. No wonder so many cop marriages went bad.

As he pulled into the driveway of his old house, he thought of Paul's comments when they'd parted at a gas station. Max had thanked his stepfather for helping him, and Paul had assured him it was no problem. "By the way," he'd said. "Your lady friend out there is a lot more than what you told your mother and me."

"What did I tell you?" Max asked.

"Not much," Paul drawled. "And there's a whole lot there."

"Are you telling me to watch that redhead temper?"

"I'm telling you to watch the redhead passion."

"Passion is not a word I would use to connect me and Zoe Barlow."

Paul grinned. "Just remember you heard it here first."

"Good night, Dad," Max said.

"Good night. Be sure and tell your mother to drive home safely."

"Will do." Paul's comments stayed with Max all the way to his house, where he found his mother watching television.

Donna Fielding looked up when she heard the door shut. "Hi, honey. Did you get everything moved?"

Max nodded and tugged his shirttail free of his jeans. "How's Annabelle?"

"Perfectly wonderful," Donna said, smiling. "She went right to sleep, and from the looks of you, you should do the same."

"I am pretty beat."

"Do you need some help tomorrow? We can set up the playpen and the cabin, and I can give you a hand putting things away."

Max thought about Zoe's comment about accepting all help when it came to moving. "Sure, Mom. I can use all the help I can get."

"Good," Donna said, smiling. "I can meet Zoe and the boys. They sound wonderful."

The memory of Danny complaining about not having a grandma resurfaced. Max had a sneaking suspicion that once his mother made the acquaintance of the Barlow boys, she would shower them with all the kindnesses and gifts she did Annabelle. Danny might just have himself a grandma after all. He just hoped she and

Paul weren't reading more into this move than there really was.

He kissed his mom on the cheek, sent her on her way, took a quick shower and fell into bed. He fell asleep almost instantly and dreamed of a passionate Zoe Barlow.

Chapter Five

As it turned out, Max's mother wasn't able to help him the next day because Annabelle was beyond cranky. Donna suspected the baby was cutting teeth and decided to keep her at home to watch her, just to make sure. For the next few days, Max packed at night, worked in the mornings and moved his things to the farm in the afternoons. By Friday, he was ready to spend the night in his new home. He'd spend the weekend getting settled and start back to work on Monday, when Zoe would start watching Annabelle.

Since Annabelle's two new teeth had come through and she was feeling better, Max's mother came to get her first look at the place. As the minicaravan passed Zoe's, he saw her in the huge vegetable garden, wearing a floppy-brimmed straw hat, obviously gathering vegetables. He'd been in such a hurry every time he'd brought out a load that he hadn't stopped, and there had been no more neighborly visits with her bearing cold drinks. Now, as she lifted a hand to wave, he realized that he'd missed seeing her and the boys. He'd already come to terms with the fact that he was spending entirely too much time thinking about her and how enticing the long shapely length of her legs were. He pushed those thoughts from his mind and pulled into the parking space at the rear of the cabin. His mother pulled in beside him and exited her vehicle, wearing a wide smile of approval.

"It's wonderful, Max."

"You haven't even seen it yet."

"I've seen enough to know it's wonderful," she said, hugging him and looping an arm around his waist. "Let's get Annabelle and see how she likes her new home."

Max disengaged Annabelle from the car seat. She'd always liked being outdoors, even when she was a newborn, and since the weather had grown warmer, his mom spent a fair amount of time outside with Annabelle in her playpen or just carrying her around and letting her look at things. Max never seemed to have enough time to do the same.

You've never taken the time.

The tiny voice inside him made the subtle correction to his thoughts. He realized with a guilty start that the voice was right. He was always eager to get her home, fed and put to bed, so that his responsibility to her was done—hopefully until morning. Now he realized there was no reason he couldn't have set up her playpen outside while he sat drinking his tea in the evenings. Having her spend time outside with him was one thing he could do.

Now, Annabelle tipped back her head and looked up at the sunlit canopy of trees above her, pointing. When she looked at him and her grandmother, the expression on her face was pure enchantment. "Da da," she said, pointing and smiling broadly.

"I see." he said, smiling back. "That's a tree, Annabelle. Say, tree. Tree."

She said something that was a far cry from "tree" and pointed to the bright splash of flowers that edged the cabin.

"Flowers," Max said, enunciating clearly. "Flowers. Pret-ty. Flow-ers."

Instead of trying to say the word, she smiled and began to blink her eyes at him, clearly trying to flutter her eyelashes. He shot his mother a questioning look. Donna laughed. "She recognized the word pretty. I've taught her to show me her pretty eyes, which means she flutters her eyelashes."

"Da da eysss," she said, almost poking her finger in Max's eye.

"She wants you to do it," Donna said. Max looked at his mother as if she were crazy. "Go ahead, macho cop man. There's no one to see you but me and Annabelle, and she isn't telling anyone. Come on, Max. Show the baby your pretty eyes."

Feeling like a complete idiot, Max looked at Annabelle and batted his eyelashes at her. To his surprise, Annabelle smiled and planted a sloppy kiss on his cheek, as if to thank him. Max had learned his lesson. He wasn't about to be responsible for breaking her good mood by scolding her for the messy kiss. Instead, he smiled at her, thanked her and gave her a kiss back.

"Ke ku," Annabelle said.

"That's thank you," his mother explained. "She's really starting to pick up words the last couple of weeks, and she's trying so hard to communicate. It won't be long before she'll be able to tell you what's wrong, what she wants, why she's crying."

"One giant step for mankind," Max said.

"Just give her a chance, Max," Donna said. "Like you just did. She's really a very good baby."

"I'll do my best."

"I know you will."

Zoe took the basket of vegetables into the mudroom to wash away the dirt in the deep sink before taking them into the kitchen. She would take some of her bounty to Max and his mother, so they could have a nice fresh salad for lunch. A sudden thought hit her. Did he like salad? And was that his mother? A woman had waved at her, but there was no way she could tell how old the female driver was. Well, there was only one way to find out, she thought, putting the onions and radishes into a bowl and carrying everything to the kitchen. She'd just go see.

As she filled the sink with cold water to wash the lettuce, she couldn't help thinking about Max. She'd given her reaction to him a lot of thought the past few days and knew that her attraction to him was all wrong. No matter how much his smile might make her heart race, no matter how aware she was of him as a man, she knew the fascination was not something she should pursue, for more reasons than she could count on both hands. He wasn't her type.

Neither was David.

True. She'd always gone for a more rugged, macho

type until David had teased and joked his way into her life. For the most part, life with him had been calm and peaceful. Five years older than she, David was easy-going by nature and supremely secure in who and what he was. He'd had the patience to deal with her youthful angst and anger, and his steady hand had gone a long way in helping her to grow up and out of some of her more troublesome inclinations.

In comparison, Max was too wounded. Whatever he'd experienced as a cop was bound to be why he seldom smiled, part of the reason for the intensity that radiated from him. And then there was the fact that he and Annabelle had been abandoned—there was no other word for it—by his wife. Cara, Zoe had heard him call her. Cara. Heart. From all Zoe had observed, Cara Murdock had no heart and she had ripped her husband's to shreds. As appealing as he might be, Zoe didn't have the time or desire to try to repair the damage. She'd long ago outgrown the need to try to save the world, and she no longer had the patience to solve someone else's problems or tiptoe around their emotional needs. She had enough trouble dealing with her own.

To further sour the idea of Max as a potential man in her life was the irrefutable fact that he was uncomfortable with his own child, and she came with three, which would only make him crazy, even though he'd dealt with her sons just fine—in small doses. The boys were already half in love with him—or the idea of a man in their lives—and she couldn't gamble with their emotions, even if she was willing to gamble with hers. She didn't want them hurt by her actions or mistakes. So even if she were willing to try to overcome the other obstacles, the boys were one she couldn't ig-

nore. The most important reason she shouldn't get involved with Max was that she had decided that her attraction was purely sexual, and therefore taboo. She'd
never been promiscuous and didn't intend to become
so just because Max Murdock was such a delicious
temptation.

Twenty minutes later, she neared the cabin. Max,
who was carrying Annabelle, and a tall woman with
short, dark brown hair were still walking around the
yard, looking at this and that. Zoe saw the woman pointing to the clematis vine sprawling across the front porch
roof. Not wanting them to feel as if they'd been sneaked
up on, she called out a cheery greeting. Both Max and
the woman turned. Zoe wasn't even aware that she'd
been holding her breath until she felt it whoosh from her
body. First, Max was as attractive as she remembered—
maybe more so—and second, the woman, though very
attractive herself, was older and looked a lot like him.
Surely she was his mother. They both waved, but she
saw that Max wasn't smiling. Her heart stopped beating; her footsteps faltered. Then he did smile, and she
felt a rush of heat sweep through her in what was rapidly becoming a standard reaction. Was it her imagination, or was that pleasure she saw in his dark eyes?

"You must be Zoe," the woman said, her expression
warm as she extended a welcoming hand.

Zoe dragged her gaze from Max long enough to take
the proffered hand. The older woman's handshake was
firm, warm. "Yes, I'm Zoe. And you're Max's mother."
She said it with confidence, since the resemblance was
unmistakable. Unable to help herself, she glanced once
more at Max, who was watching the exchange with a
look of interest on his face.

"Yes," the woman said, "but please call me Donna."

"Donna." Zoe held out the basket. "I brought you some fresh lettuce and things from the garden and a chicken potpie I had in the freezer. I thought you could make a salad and have one less meal to worry about while you're getting Max and Annabelle settled in."

She glanced again at Max and realized he was making a slow survey of her body. A flush started at her toes and moved slowly over her, seeming to settle in the very heart of her femininity. His gaze finally found hers. There was unmistakable look in his eyes, an awareness so intense it took Zoe's breath away. So much for getting her attraction in perspective! She forced her gaze from the heat in his eyes and turned her attention to Annabelle.

"Hey, cutie," she said, chucking the baby under the chin and hoping Max's mother didn't notice the effect her son was having on his new landlady.

Annabelle smiled and leaned forward, her arms outstretched toward Zoe, who took her from her father with a soft burst of laughter. As the exchange was made, Zoe sneaked another look at Max. There was nothing in his eyes but surprise at the baby's actions.

"I think she likes you," Donna said.

"She came right to me the other day, too," Zoe said, smiling.

"That was one of the reasons I thought this move might be a good thing," Max said to his mother. "I figured if Annabelle liked Zoe, half the problem was solved."

Zoe's glance met his over the baby's head. Again, there was that intangible something she couldn't read in his eyes.

"It helps, all right," his mother said. "Why don't we go inside? I can put this basket of goodies down and you can show me the cabin."

"Oh, I can't stay," Zoe said. "I have lots of weeding to do."

"Surely you have time for a glass of tea," Donna said. "I, for one, don't mind postponing the last of the unpacking, and I'm sure Max doesn't mind, either."

"I'll take a glass of tea," Max said, heading toward the front door. "But if you ladies don't mind, I'll put the baby bed together while you get acquainted. If I know Annabelle, she'll be ready for her nap as soon as she finishes lunch. I want it to be ready for her."

"We don't mind at all, do we, Zoe?" Donna said.

Though she didn't want to seem pushy to Max, Zoe didn't know how to refuse his mother's invitation without sounding unsociable. "Of course not, but I really can't stay long."

"Thirty minutes," Donna said, gesturing toward the porch.

Settling Annabelle on her hip, Zoe followed Max and his mother inside. Donna went into the kitchen to get the iced tea, and Zoe took the opportunity to look around. She was eager to see what he'd done to the cabin, hoping she could get some clue as to what made the man tick. The sofa and chair she'd loaned him looked great in the rustic setting. He'd brought in an oak bookshelf that was full of what looked like reference and research type books, along with some Robert B. Parker and John Sandford novels. He'd hung some pictures. Inspecting the one hanging over the fireplace more closely, she was surprised to see it was a signed and numbered McCarthy print featuring Native Americans. The others looked like the same artist. She had to commend his taste. McCarthy was highly collectible.

She turned and looked at the dining area. A bowl of fruit sat on the table. No frilly flowers for the former cop. Annabelle's high chair, complete with a clean bib on the tray, sat in the corner, ready to be used.

"It looks great," she said to Max. "I'm glad the couch and chair work so well."

"It does look good, doesn't it?" he said, placing his hands on his lean hips and surveying his new domain with obvious pleasure. "Thanks for the loan."

Though he smiled, there was no lingering hint of the heat in his eyes she'd seen there just moments ago. "You're more than welcome. They certainly weren't doing me any good stuck off in the spare bedroom."

"I saw you looking at the prints. What do you think?"

"I think they're wonderful, though I was a bit surprised to see them."

"Surprised that a lowly cop collects Western art, or surprised that he collects any kind of art?"

"Both, I think," Zoe said, truthfully.

"Ah," he said, nodding. "That rare creature. An honest woman."

"Is that how you really feel?" Zoe asked, more curious than offended by the comment.

"What? That most women aren't honest?" he asked. "Actually, I'm not sure much of mankind is honest."

"That's a pretty cynical way of thinking."

"If you'd seen what I've seen on the streets, you'd be a little cynical, too," he told her, his lips tightening. "I've seen mothers selling their eleven-year-old daughters for crack, kids who steal from their parents for some meth—" He broke off and gave a dismissive wave of his hand. "Sorry. You don't want to hear about all that ugly stuff. Your life is far removed from it and if you're very lucky, it always will be."

"I hope so," she told him, dismayed by the angry frustration she'd seen in his eyes.

Zoe was thankful that Donna chose that moment to return, bearing a tray with three glasses of iced tea and a plate of cookies.

"Here we go," she said in a cheerful voice. "Max, honey, why don't you put Annabelle in her high chair. I found her teething biscuits, and I brought her some apple juice." She smiled at Zoe. "Annabelle isn't too little to join in our woman's talk, is she?"

"Not at all," Zoe said. As Max approached to take his daughter, Zoe held her out at arm's length. She didn't want a repeat of the last time they'd switched the baby. No way she wanted to feel Max's hand against her breasts. *Liar.* She felt the heat of embarrassment sweep over her face at the maverick thought. Maybe Max was right. Maybe the world was filled with untruthful people. She'd certainly become expert at lying to herself.

Max put Annabelle in her high chair, took a glass of tea, nabbed a couple of cookies and disappeared through the kitchen door. Donna gave the baby her biscuit and juice before offering Zoe a chocolate chip cookie. "They're homemade."

"I can tell," Zoe said, taking one and putting it on the saucer. "They look delicious."

"Do you bake?" Donna said, helping herself to a cookie.

"I do. I like baking and cooking, though I don't often get the chance to make anything fancy. The boys seem to be typical meat-and-potatoes boys. Except Danny," she added with a smile. "Danny is strictly a peanut-butter-and-jelly boy."

"Max and his brother Ryan were that way, too, until they got a little older." Her hostess propped an elbow on the table and rested her chin in her hand, leaning toward Zoe eagerly. "Tell me about them."

Zoe spent the next few minutes telling Donna about the boys, doing her best not to drag things out indefinitely, which was tempting, since her audience seemed to be truly interested.

"And how long have you been widowed?"

Before she could answer, Max came through the kitchen carrying parts of Annabelle's baby bed. Their gazes clashed briefly, before he continued toward her bedroom, and Zoe's heart did another of those annoying little backflips. "Three years."

"Not all that long."

"No." *Not so long, but sometimes it seems like an eternity.* Like now, when her body was flushed and she found herself aching for the touch of a man's hands. Max's hands.

"I can empathize," Donna said, drawing Zoe's attention back to the conversation. "Max's dad was killed in the line of duty."

Zoe couldn't hide her surprise. "He was a soldier?"

Donna shook her head. "A cop. He was killed trying to settle a domestic disturbance."

"I'm so sorry," Zoe said.

Donna's eyes misted over. She reached out and gave Zoe's hand a pat. "Thank you. It's been a long time, and I was lucky enough to find another wonderful man, but some days I still miss him."

"How long before you married again?" Zoe asked. Her gaze followed Max as he passed through the dining area to get another load from the car. She wasn't sure why she'd asked the question, because every person and every situation were different, but somehow, she felt a connection with Donna Fielding and felt there would be a certain validity in whatever Max's mother told her.

"Four years," she said.

Zoe took a swallow of tea and decided to ask the question, even though it, too, had a different answer for every person asked. "Was it easy for your boys to accept another man in their father's place?"

"There was never any overt disapproval. Paul is a very likable man, and Max and Ryan knew how hard it had been on me trying to provide for them, so they were fairly accepting when we told them. Paul made it very clear that he wasn't there to take Lowell's place. He told them he wanted to make his own place in the family. It took a while, especially for Max, who was very close to his dad, but he and Paul have grown very close over the years."

"That's wonderful," Zoe said sincerely. "My friend keeps telling me I'll find someone else, but with three boys, it seems impossible to me that anyone would want to take on all of us." Her eyes held earnest conviction as they met Donna's. "I don't want to make a mistake. I don't want to add a divorce to the emotional load the kids and I already have."

"Unfortunately, you and I both know there are no guarantees," Donna said. "Life and love come with a certain amount of risk. If you'd like a bit of advice, I'd tell you not to rush into anything and use your instincts. They're more often right than wrong."

That was the problem. While she was very attracted to Max Murdock, all her instincts told her that even if he shared that attraction, he wasn't the right man for her. But knowing that didn't change the way her heart picked up speed whenever she saw him, or the way her body reminded her of the length of her abstinence whenever he smiled that rare, lethal smile.

"What if you aren't sure you can trust those instincts?" she asked. "What if you meet someone you don't feel is right, but that attraction is there?"

"Exercise the greatest caution," Donna said with a smile. "But on the other hand, just because someone isn't like the first person you loved doesn't mean they're wrong for you. It just means they're different. As long as your basic values and approach to life are the same, you can probably work out the other kinks."

"I hadn't thought about that. David was a lot different from the type of men I'd dated. At first, I wasn't sure he was right for me at all."

"I felt the same way about Paul. Max and Ryan's father was far more physical, rougher around the edges, probably from the kind of work he did. He loved football and boxing. Until he retired, Paul worked in an office. The most violence he saw was on the evening news, and the only sport he really likes is golf. But he went to every baseball, football or basketball game Ryan and Max played in. Like Lowell did, Paul has a great capacity for love, and he's a very giving person. We share the same values. Those are the kinds of differences I'm talking about."

"Da da," Annabelle said, pointing to Max who was passing through again.

"Yes, that's Daddy," Donna said, handing the baby

another teething biscuit. She'd managed to smear the first one from ear to ear.

"Are you talking about me again?" Max had paused in the doorway. The question was accompanied by a teasing smile. It was a side of him Zoe hadn't seen.

"Actually, I was telling Zoe about your father and Paul," Donna said.

"I was lucky to have them both," he said.

Unable to take much more time in the same room with him, Zoe glanced at her watch. "I really need to go," she said, directing the statement to Max's mother as she pushed back her chair and stood. "The weeds are growing as I sit here."

Donna rose. "I understand, but I'm glad we had the chance to visit a while."

"Me, too," Zoe said in all sincerity. She turned to Max. "I've been trying to keep the boys away, but I feel I should warn you that they'll want to come over and say hello to you and Annabelle when they get out of school, since they know you're moving today."

"That's fine." He held up a hand, and turned toward his bedroom. "Don't go until I give you my phone number. I'll be right back."

She nodded and turned to Donna with a wry smile. "They've taken quite a liking to Max and Annabelle— even though she is a girl—and I'm afraid they'll make nuisances of themselves if I don't keep a tight rein on them."

"I can hardly wait to meet them," Donna said.

Zoe smiled. "You may change your tune when you do. They can be a handful."

"Can't they all?" Donna said as Max reappeared in the doorway.

He handed Zoe a piece of paper. "That's my number. Call if anything comes up with Annabelle, or if you need me for anything."

Zoe tucked the small slip of yellow paper into her shorts pocket. "I will." She was almost to the door when Donna called, "Is it all right if I give the boys some juice and cookies?"

"They'd love you forever," Zoe said, warmed by the gesture. She gave another wave and left, thinking that if Max Murdock had any of his mother's qualities, he must be an okay guy.

"Miss Donna is great!" Chris said when they returned from the cabin.

"She's just like Grandma," Danny said. "She gave us cookies and juice, and she read a story to us and Annabelle."

"It was a baby story," Chris said, "so I went to help Max put his books and things away. He tried to pay me for helping, but I told him no. I told him that's what neighbors did. Help each other. Oh, and I asked him if he'd come to my Little League game tomorrow. He said he had a lot to do, but he'd think about it."

Zoe gave an inward groan. She couldn't believe Chris had asked Max that. It was even less believable that Max said he might go.

"I asked him if he could put the chain back on my bike," Mike offered. "He said he would when he found his tools."

"Oh, Mike!" Zoe cried in dismay. "I said I'd fix it."

"Yeah," Mike said. "About a year ago."

"It's more like a couple of weeks," Zoe said, "but your point is taken."

"I thought if neighbors help each other out, then he'd be glad to do it," Mike told her.

Zoe sighed. She hated it when her truisms came back to haunt her. "I'm sure he won't mind this time, but you boys have to remember that he works at home, and you can't make a nuisance of yourselves."

"What's that?" Danny asked.

"You can't be going to Max's house and bothering him about every little thing."

"What kind of work does he do?" Mike asked.

"He writes books for grown-ups," Zoe told him, "and writing is the kind of work where you really have to concentrate. If you just drop in, you'll interrupt his train of thought. You'll have to get in the habit of doing your visiting in the evenings or on the weekends. If he doesn't work then," she added. "Do you understand?"

The boys all nodded, but she thought they looked saddened by the directive. "Good. Now, go on out and play while I start dinner."

She watched them go, sadly. The boys were certainly enamored of Max, whom they no doubt saw as the father figure they so desperately needed. Her heart ached for them, but there was nothing she could do about the void in their lives that David's death had brought about. As if that weren't enough to worry about, it seemed Max's mother stood a good chance of becoming a surrogate grandmother. On one hand, she was thrilled that Donna Fielding was caring enough to want to befriend her children; on the other, she couldn't help wondering what would happen when Max and Annabelle moved.

And it would happen, sooner or later. Zoe wasn't in the habit of deceiving herself. She knew that even if the arrangement turned out to be long-term, Max would eventually outgrow the cabin. Worst-case scenario: he would find another woman he wanted to share his life with and the new family would need a bigger place. What would happen to the boys then? How would they deal with the loss of both these people when the inevitable happened?

Zoe told herself not to borrow trouble. It was too late to change the course she'd taken. She'd just have to hope he stayed a while and pray she could deal with his leaving in a way the boys would understand when it came time for the separation.

"This is very good chicken potpie," Donna said that evening as she, Max and Annabelle sat at the small dining table. "It was thoughtful of Zoe to bring it over."

"It's excellent," Max agreed, nodding. "I'm not sure when I've had a salad that tasted this good."

"That's because the greens really are fresh," his mother told him. She mashed up a piece of potato with a couple of green peas and gave Annabelle a bite on the tip of her spoon.

"Mmm," Annabelle said.

Donna laughed. "Even Annabelle thinks it's good."

Max smiled and helped himself to more of the potpie. "Smart kid."

"I liked her."

"I thought you would," Max said without elaborating.

"It sounds as if she's been through a lot, and becoming a widow at twenty-nine doesn't seem to have made her angry at the world or bitter in any way."

"Unlike other people who shall remain nameless," Max said, his eyes filled with mockery.

Donna refused to take that particular bait. "I think this move will be good for you. There's a wonderful feel out here, and the boys will be good for Annabelle." She smiled, "They're adorable, aren't they?"

Max cocked one eyebrow in inquiry. "Adorable isn't the word I'd use. Cute, maybe. Ornery, most definitely. Well brought up, undoubtedly."

Donna smiled and offered Annabelle another bite. "I was surprised to hear you say you'd go to Chris's ball game tomorrow."

"I said I would if I had time," Max corrected.

"Let me tell you something that would be important to remember. Kids never hear the word *if.* He'll be devastated if you don't show up," Donna told him.

Max shook his head. "I'll never get the hang of how to deal with kids."

"You will if you work at it, and if you accept Annabelle for who and what she is and don't expect any more from her than she's able to give."

"I know who she is. She's mine and Cara's daughter."

"And therein lies part of the problem," Donna said cryptically.

"What do you mean?"

"She's a constant reminder of Cara. How can she not be?"

"I don't blame Annabelle for that," Max said in a testy tone.

"Not consciously. But it's there. What you have to do is look at Annabelle as the very best parts of you both, not as a reminder of how Cara walked out on you. Remember that she walked out on Annabelle, too. You may not realize it now, but she's going to have to deal with that later, when she's old enough to understand what happened. You'll need to be there to help her understand that Cara's leaving wasn't her fault any more than it was yours."

"I could have been a better husband."

"Most of us could be better mates," Donna said with a dismissive shrug. "You were gone a lot. Maybe you weren't always there when she wanted you to be. And there's no doubt you worked a dangerous job. Maybe you weren't as open as she'd have liked you to be, but that's part of the work you did. What I saw was a man who always brought home a paycheck, always supported her efforts, always did everything in his power to give her what she wanted. If you'd been a millionaire, it would never have been enough, Max. Cara's problem was her own lack of self-worth. Money can't fix that. Neither can smothering the people you love and expecting them to be your crutch."

"So it was all Cara's fault?"

"I didn't say that. What I am saying is that if you want to start healing, you have to cut yourself some slack."

He gave a thoughtful nod. "Maybe." After several seconds, he said, "And you think Zoe will be good for Annabelle?"

"I think Zoe will be good for both of you."

His eyes narrowed in suspicion. "I hope that statement doesn't mean what I think it does."

"All I meant was that she seems decent and caring. It never hurts anyone to be around that kind of person. What and who you deal with every day makes an impression on you, no matter how much you'd like to think it doesn't," his mother said. "In the case of law enforcement people, I think it makes you suspicious, a little hardened and wary. I saw it happen to your father, and I saw it happening to you before you quit the force."

Max scrubbed a hand down the side of his face. "I have rubbed elbows with the dregs of humanity in the past several years. Now I'm writing about it. You know, it's almost like a purge."

"Then it will be good for you, just as Zoe and her boys will be good for you. You'll absorb this world just as you did the world you lived in before, and it will make its impression on you."

"So my environment will change me, make me a better person?" he asked, facetiously.

Donna smiled. "There's nothing wrong with you as a person. You're good and decent and you have a tender heart. You've just hidden it away as a form of protection."

He gave her an indulgent smile. "My mom, the shrink. And that's all that's behind your thinking Zoe will be good for me? Just that I'll—what? Mellow out or something?"

"Or something," she said. "And yes, that's all. But if you did find yourself becoming…interested in her in another way, I wouldn't have a problem with it."

Max couldn't hide his amazement. "Unbelievable. You'd be happy if I became romantically involved with Zoe Barlow. And you base this on a twenty-minute conversation with the woman?" His voice held incredulity.

"I saw the way you looked at her."

"And how was that?" Max asked resting his elbow on the table and leaning forward in interest.

"Like you were trying not to look at her." Donna's

smile was serene. "As I've told you before, you have good instincts, Max. Where on earth do you think you got them?"

Chapter Six

On Saturday morning, Max awakened slowly, to the sound of a bird singing outside his bedroom window, which he'd left open in order to absorb the rich rural fragrances and intriguing country sounds. He drew in a deep hyacinth-scented breath and, stretching mightily, rested his head on his crossed forearms and closed his eyes again. Being in a strange place and sleeping in a strange bed, he'd expected to lie awake for hours. Instead, he'd crashed the minute his head hit the pillow. Thankfully, so had Annabelle. He turned his head and glanced at the bedside clock. Six-thirty and she was still asleep. It was a miracle, of sorts.

Max closed his eyes again, savoring the moment of quiet. It had been a hectic week, and he knew the next one wouldn't be much better as he and Annabelle settled into their new routine. Like his mother, he thought

Zoe and her boys would be good for Annabelle. He wasn't quite as certain Zoe would be good for him. His reasoning had a lot to do with the fact that he thought of her as an attractive woman, not his daughter's baby-sitter, and his feeling that he wasn't ready to feel any-thing for any woman. But ready or not, his mom had been right when she'd said he'd tried hard not to look at Zoe. It was unbelievable that his interest was so ob-vious. He gave a growl of irritation. He was thirty-four and had been around the block a couple of times, yet he hadn't felt so gauche and untried since high school.

What was it about Zoe Barlow—besides those long, shapely legs—that drew him? Something about her called out to him in ways he'd never experienced. It was more than a realization that she was extremely pretty and had a wholesomeness that was, in its own way, sexy. Unlike his mother, Max wasn't so good at analyz-ing things. At least, not emotions and personal matters. A crime scene was something else. Okay, he thought with a sigh. He was willing to acknowledge that whether he liked it or not, he was attracted to Zoe. The question was what to do about it.

He decided on nothing, for the moment. Attraction to the opposite sex was normal, especially when a per-son had been through a lengthy period of abstinence. He could accept that. What he couldn't accept was get-ting involved. Even if Zoe was the kind of woman he was usually drawn to—which she wasn't—the timing was all wrong. He had too much riding on this book to have his thoughts torn between his work and a woman. He didn't have time for an affair. He certainly didn't have time for a full-fledged relationship.

A sudden thought hit him. If his mother had noticed

his preoccupation with Zoe, had she? If she had, what was she thinking? Or—and here was a scary thought—was she attracted to him, too? He *knew* she'd felt something the day her hand had been caught between Annabelle's body and his chest. He'd heard her soft gasp and seen the sudden confusion in her eyes. And there was no mistaking the look he'd seen in her eyes the day before, when he'd caught himself giving her the once-over. Surprise. Awareness. A dreamy sexuality.

He thought of Zoe's long smooth legs and felt an undeniable desire to trail his fingertips from the soles of her feet to the edge of her shorts and beyond, just to see if her skin was as silky as it looked. She had a beautiful complexion, the kind women longed for. Creamy. Flawless except for the light spattering of whiskey-colored freckles that danced across the bridge of her nose and over the curve of her cheekbones. He wondered if there were freckles on her shoulders…the swell of her breasts…and beyond….

Max's body responded in typical male fashion to the images that drifted through his mind like wisps of smoke. Tantalizing. Elusive. Mysterious. Assaulting his senses and eroding his will with their very ambiguousness. Making his body war with his mind, his emotions with his intellect, insanity with logic. But when, he asked himself, had the heart ever listened to the mind? When had common sense ever won out over desire? In his experience, it was only after being in a relationship for a while that wisdom began to assert itself and the mind started weighing the pros and cons. The prudent thing to do would be to keep their relationship impersonal and not let his emotions become involved. It was a good plan, if he could stick to it.

A sound from the other room told him Annabelle was waking up. Fearing she would be frightened waking up in strange surroundings, he swung his legs to the side of the bed and sat up. Maybe if he got to her before she began to cry, she'd be in a good mood.

He pulled on a pair of shorts and headed toward her room, expecting her to be standing in her crib, waiting for him to rescue her from behind the bars that confined her. Instead, she was lying on her side, examining the clean but tattered terry cloth rabbit Danny had given her the evening before. A good fifteen inches long and no bigger around than a quarter, its name was Skinny Rabbit. In a solemn voice, Danny had told Max and his mother that Skinny Rabbit had been his favorite toy when he was a baby, and he wanted Annabelle to have it now that he was too old to play with it. To Danny's delight, Annabelle, who already had one rabbit she liked to chew on, had grabbed the offering and carried it directly to her mouth.

Now, seeing Max in the doorway, Annabelle clamped her teeth on to one of the rabbit's ears, rolled to her knees and pulled herself up, grinning at him around the dangling stuffed animal. Max couldn't help the chuckle that escaped him. She looked so cute standing there in her diaper and T-shirt, the long rabbit hanging out of her mouth like a retriever with its catch. Something in her manner reminded him of his brother, and it came to him with something of a jolt that Murdock blood really did run in her veins. As his mom had reminded him, she was both Cara's and his.

Hearing the sound of his laughter, Annabelle's smile grew even wider, and she began to bounce up and down in the crib. Once again feeling that subtle but undeniable connection he'd felt once or twice lately, Max sauntered over. His mother's advice ran through his mind. He should accept Annabelle for what she was and where she was in her development. Right now, that was easy to do. No one with a heart could deny that she was adorable, and he strongly suspected she knew it.

As he approached the crib, she snatched the rabbit from her mouth and held out her arms for him to pick her up, which he did, planting a kiss on her chubby cheek. She surprised him by opening her mouth wide and kissing him back. A little wet, but slobber was washable, and the heartfelt token of her affection was, as the credit card ad claimed, priceless.

"Are you hungry?" he asked, as if she could answer. "Do you want Daddy to fix you something to eat?"

"Mmm," she said, obviously making the connection with eat and good. Again, Max realized that they were communicating. In the scheme of things, it wasn't much, but to him, it was a major accomplishment.

"Let's go have breakfast," he said, talking to her as if she were an adult. "Then we'll take a bath and call Zoe to see what time Chris's ball game starts. I have a feeling you and I will be going to a Little League game at some point today."

Annabelle smiled, as if the idea pleased her.

Zoe was putting bread in the toaster when the phone rang. Expecting it to be Celia, she said, "Joe's mule barn."

"Excuse me," a masculine voice said. "I was calling the Barlow residence."

Recognizing Max's voice, Zoe felt her face flame with embarrassment. "This is the Barlow residence, Max. I thought you were Celia."

He actually chuckled. She hadn't heard him laugh before, and the effect the low, sexy sound had on her libido was instant and way beyond potent.

"Somehow, I never expected you to be a phone cutup."

"Don't tell the boys," Zoe said, smiling. "I'm always talking to them about phone etiquette." Knowing he hadn't called to chitchat, she asked, "Is there something I can do for you?"

"I was calling about Chris's baseball game. I don't know if he told you or not, but he asked me if I wanted to come."

"He did mention it, and I told him he shouldn't bother you with that sort of thing. I'm sure you have plenty to do ."

"Sure I do, but it will be here whenever I get to it."

Zoe's heart began took a slight dip. Was he actually going to go watch Chris play ball? "Don't feel as if you have to go if you don't want to."

"Would you rather I didn't?" he asked.

Would she? She wasn't sure. Somehow, this seemed to be a step in a direction away from tenant and landlady. "No, why?"

"That's the second way out you've offered."

"No! It's fine that you go. I guess you took me by surprise by taking Chris up on his invitation."

"Well, it took me a bit by surprise, too, but this is a new start, in a way, so it made sense for me to do something I normally wouldn't do. I played college ball, so it's a game I like, but I haven't been to a Little League game since I was a kid. I'm looking forward to it."

"It will be an experience," Zoe said.

"What position does he play?"

"Second base."

"Is he any good?"

Zoe heard the teasing note in his voice and decided that a Max Murdock in full seduction mode would be hard to disregard. He was difficult enough to resist as it was. "This is his mother," she teased back. "What do you expect me to say? Of course, he's good."

Max laughed, then said, "You realize that if I go I'll have to take Annabelle. I might need a little help."

"I'd be glad to give you a hand," Zoe told him. "She'll probably like all the noise and excitement."

"Probably so. What all should I take?"

"Besides the usual?" Zoe said "Something for her to drink, some snacks, like Cheerios or something, a few toys that can be washed off if she drops them in the dirt and her stroller."

"I could go out of town for the weekend with less," Max said dryly. "So what time are you leaving? I'll need to follow you, since I don't know the way."

"The game is at eleven. We'll need to leave here in an hour."

"I'm going to have to get a move on if I want to make it," Max said.

"I'd ask you and Annabelle to ride with us, but I don't think I can get her car seat in with the three boys in back."

"Why don't you ride with us? There's plenty of room in the Expedition."

Zoe was more than a little surprised by the offer. What should she do? If she said no, the boys would never forgive her. If she accepted, was she taking their acquaintance across some kind of imaginary boundary into a different sort of relationship than either she or

Max planned—or wanted? "We'd love to ride with you," she heard herself saying.

"Great," Max said. "Annabelle and I will see you in about an hour, then."

"Max!" she said before he could hang up.

"Yeah?"

"Thank you for doing this. It will mean a lot to Chris."

"No problem," he said and broke the connection.

After she'd done the same, Zoe stood staring at the phone. What had she just done? She could tell herself any neighbors would do the same thing, and she would be right. The problem was that no matter how much she might believe the attraction she felt for Max was just a normal reaction of a woman to an attractive, sexy man, it didn't alter the fact that her feelings for him were far from neighborly.

Not only was Chris thrilled, the other boys were extremely excited that not only was Max going to watch the game, they were all going together. Despite the fact that they got off to a little bit of a late start, Max managed to get them there just as Chris's coach was sending the team out onto the field for practice. Chris settled his hat on his head, grabbed his bag and leaped out of the SUV in a dead run, yelling that he'd see them later. Mike and Danny, who also played ball but on two other teams, stayed behind to help carry lawn chairs, the baby paraphernalia and Annabelle.

"I'll carry her," Mike said when Max unfastened the car seat harness.

"I want to carry her," Danny said, poking his lower lip out in a pout.

"I'm going to carry her and the diaper bag," Zoe said. "Mike, you and Danny each carry a chair. Max can get the other chair and the stroller." She looked at Max. "Okay?"

He sketched a little salute. "Yes, ma'am,"

"Sorry. I didn't mean to boss you, but it seemed the logical division of duties."

"Works for me," Max told her, handing Annabelle over. While he unloaded the rest of their things, Zoe talked to Annabelle, who was fascinated by the gold studs in Zoe's ears. "Have you thought about getting her ears pierced?" she asked Max.

He looked at her as if she'd just asked if he'd thought about the possibility of sending his daughter to the moon. "No, I have not," he said in a firm voice. He settled his sunglasses on the bridge of his straight nose with a no-nonsense gesture. "She's just a baby."

"They say that's the best time to do it," Zoe told him, wishing he hadn't put on the glasses so she could gauge the expression in his eyes better. "Actually, they say to do it as a tiny baby is even better. They don't bother their ears while they're healing."

"That's cruel."

Zoe smiled. Typical male reaction. "I just asked," she said, holding up a hand to forestall any more comments. To the baby she said, "I'll keep working on him, Annabelle." She said it loud enough that Max could hear. When he shot her a frowning glance over the top of his sunglasses, she offered him her most innocent smile.

With Annabelle on her hip, Zoe led the way to the bleachers, where Chris's team's families were settling in to watch the game. Max, Mike and Danny followed, carrying their things. She reminded him of his mother, Max thought, seeing the patient smile that curved Zoe's lips as she promised Annabelle she would try to convince him to get the baby's ears pierced. Except he wasn't sure his mother had ever looked as hot as Zoe did. Her auburn hair was twisted up in a clasp. Loose curls tumbled in sexy disarray. She didn't look as if she was wearing much makeup. Her thick eyelashes were long and dark and her lips looked glossy—wet and ripe—reminding him of something sweet and peachy. She was wearing short denim shorts that made her legs look a mile long and a lime-green scoop-neck top that left her arms bare. The simple outfit answered one of his questions. The freckles he'd wondered about were scattered like drops of pale honey over her shoulders and as far as the top would allow him to see. Against his will, his imagination leaped to the logical conclusion. There was little doubt in his mind that the golden flecks dotted the swell of her breasts. At that moment, he'd have given half his next advance to verify his assumption. How had he ever thought she was merely wholesomely attractive?

In the next breath, he cursed himself for thinking such things. Hadn't he learned his lesson with Cara? Did he think that just because a woman was sweet and generous and had a knack for mothering, that she was any less likely to be a heartbreaker? His mind told him it was far less likely, but the heart that was still a bit bruised told him he was a fool if he believed it.

Zoe saw the frown lurking in Max's eyes and wondered if something was wrong. "Is this okay?" she asked. She was standing near the fence at a place that gave a good view of first base and home plate.

"Looks fine to me," he said, his attention focused on the moment at hand.

"Oh, good!" Mike exclaimed, dropping his bag chair to the ground. "We get the shady side today. Annabelle won't get too much sun."

Zoe bit back a smile and watched as Max helped Mike set up the chairs near the fence. When they finished, Danny was just arriving with his chair, which he was dragging through the dirt.

"Hey, Zoe!"

She glanced up into the small stand of bleachers and saw Helen Hardy, the mother of one of the boys on the team, waving. Zoe waved back. She didn't know many of the moms yet, but Hank Hardy was one of just two kids who'd been on Chris's team the previous year. Helen smiled and Zoe couldn't help noticing that she was giving Max a thorough once-over. She could only imagine what must be going through the other woman's mind, especially since Zoe was holding the baby. Let them try to do the math on this one, she thought.

She sat down in the chair, put her own sunshades on and settled Annabelle, who was chewing on a rubber duck, on her lap. Zoe pointed through the chain-link fence to Chris, who had just caught a pop-up the coach had hit to him. Without missing a beat, he zinged it to first base.

"See, Annabelle. See Chris?" Zoe asked.

Annabelle pointed toward the kids on the field and mumbled something unintelligible around the duck's head.

"He has a good arm," Max said.

"I think so." Zoe turned to look at him and pulled her glasses down so that he could see her eyes. "I think it's only fair to warn you I'm a yeller."

He pulled his glasses down with a forefinger and peered at her over the tops. "A yeller?"

"Yeah," she said, nodding. "I'll probably embarrass you."

A teasing glimmer danced in his eyes and set Zoe's nerve endings sizzling. "Fat chance."

"Don't say you haven't been warned," she said, pushing her glasses back up.

An hour and fifteen minutes later, Chris's team was called the winner. Chris had hit two doubles and a single and caught an infield pop fly. He'd had a good game.

"You did warn me," Max said, a wide smile on his face. "I'd never have believed so much noise could come out of such a classy-looking package."

Zoe wasn't sure whether she should be embarrassed that he'd acknowledged that she was loud. She was too stunned by his statement that she was a classy-looking package. "I did embarrass you."

"In case you didn't notice, I did a fair amount of yelling myself. I'd forgotten how intense games can be, even at this level."

"Yeah, I love these close ones," she said, hefting Annabelle, who'd fallen asleep in her arms, to her shoulder. To everyone's surprise, she'd been perfect, content to be passed from one to the other of her admirers, who'd entertained her until she'd finally fallen asleep on Zoe's shoulder.

Max reached out and touched the baby's dark curls. "I think she had a good time, too."

"You enjoyed it, then?"

"You bet," Max said. "You can count me in as a spectator unless the games fall during my working hours."

Zoe felt a pleased smile playing with the corners of her mouth. "Chris will be thrilled."

As if on cue, a beaming Chris ran up to them, barely able to contain his excitement. "Did you see that ball I hit to center field, Max?"

"I sure did," Max said, giving him a high five. "And that was a heck of a fly ball you caught in the fifth."

"I was afraid for a minute I wasn't going to get there in time," Chris confessed, whipping off his ball cap and scratching his sweaty head.

"And I'm afraid my arm's going to fall off is someone doesn't take Annabelle," Zoe said, half-teasing, half-serious.

Max took a step toward her when he was stopped by a jovial voice, saying "Hi there."

Everyone turned at the sound of the unfamiliar masculine voice.

"Hey coach!" Chris said, smiling.

"Good game, Chris," the coach said before extended his hand to Max. "Hi. I'm Bill Young, Chris's coach."

"Max Murdock," he said, taking the coach's hand. "Nice to meet you."

"Same to you," the coach said. "I'm glad I caught you before you left."

Max pulled off his sunglasses and put them in the pocket of his shirt. "What can I do for you?"

Zoe looked from Max to the coach, wondering what was going on. Was Coach Young a fan of Max's writing? Chris, too, was watching the exchange with shameless interest.

"Did you ever play any ball?" the coach asked Max.

"College," Max said. "S.A.U. Catcher."

"You were a catcher, Max?" Chris said. "Sweet."

The coach cast Chris a strange look, obviously wondering why he'd called Max by his first name. At that second, Zoe realized where the conversation was headed. Her heart took a nosedive, and her stunned gaze flew to Max's. Coach Young didn't know Chris's dad was dead. When he'd seen Max with her and the other children, he'd come to a logical conclusion, albeit a wrong one. She started to correct the mistake, but the coach was already talking.

"—ought to be trying Chris out as a catcher."

"He's probably right where he needs to be," Max said.

"Yeah? Coach Ron and I think he has quite a bit of ability to be a pitcher, but he needs some work if he wants to be one of our regulars."

The whole situation was getting worse by the minute. Zoe started to speak, to tell the coach that he'd made a terrible mistake, that Max wasn't Chris's father, but when she opened her mouth, Max stepped closer. "I forgot about your arm," he said. "Here. Let me take her," he said, reaching for Annabelle.

As she relinquished her precious burden, Zoe's eyes, filled with apology, met his. He looked back at her, solemnly, and said to the coach, "I can probably work some with him in the evenings."

"Great!" He gave Max a considering look. "I don't suppose you'd have time to help us with the team, would you? We could use another coach."

"I appreciate the offer," Max told him, uncomfortable for the first time, "but I don't think I'd have the time."

"Right. No problem." Suddenly, the relief on the

coach's face was transformed into an expression of chagrin. He put his hands on his hip and gave a shake of his head. "I just realized I've made a terrible mistake. You aren't Max's father, are you?"

"Regrettably, no."

"I know what you mean. I'm crazy about my step-son, too," the coach said.

"I'm not Chris's stepfather, either. I just rent a house from Mrs. Barlow, and Chris asked me to come to his game."

Bill Young's face burned red with embarrassment.

"But I really wouldn't mind working with Chris, if you'll tell me what to do."

"Setting up a fake plate and having him throw to you to improve his accuracy would be great. We can work on some other things later."

"Glad to help," Max said, extending his hand. "Nice to meet you."

"You, too."

Clearly relieved that the conversation was over, the coach made a hasty departure. Zoe's gaze met Max's. "I'm so sorry that happened."

He shrugged. "It's no big deal." He looked at the kids who were regarding him with obvious awe. "You guys ready to load up?"

They nodded in unison and picked up their desig-nated parcels.

"Let's go. I could use something cold. Maybe some ice cream," he said, shooting a questioning glance at Zoe. "My treat."

That evening, when the boys had been put to bed, Zoe sat on the front porch listening to the tree frogs and

whip-poor-wills and thinking about the day—which
Celia had demanded to hear about as soon as Zoe
walked through the front door. There had been a nostalgic sweetness to it that brought a lump to her throat.
Three years ago, she and David had been taking Chris
to ball games whenever he wasn't on duty. Having Max
go along had brought back those memories. They'd felt
like a family today, and even though she knew it was a
false feeling, she'd seen the happiness in her children's
eyes. For the first time, they could relate to their friends
whose fathers attended every game. For the first time
in a long time, they could look over and feel that they
were part of something complete, whole.

Max had been the soul of graciousness when the
coach had mistaken him for Chris's dad. While Zoe was
freaking out inside, he'd handled the situation with
ease. Only once had he lost his composure, and that had
been when the coach asked him to help coach the team.
Consenting to help Chris was one thing; committing to
coaching a Little League team was something else altogether. Maybe that was a little too much like family
for Max's comfort.

Zoe pushed the glider with one foot and closed her
eyes, reliving the moment he'd taken Annabelle from
her. It was such a familiar scene, one she'd experienced
hundreds of times with David, but there was no way she
could ever confuse one man for the other. Easygoing
David had been the epitome of wholesome American
male. Kind. Forgiving. Loving. Max had an edge to
him. A hint of roughness. A suggestion of danger. Other
than to answer questions, he didn't talk much. It was
almost as if he were afraid that by opening up, he might
reveal too much of himself. Instead, he watched and lis-

tened. Not only did he hear and sift everything said around him, he noticed every gesture, every blink of an eye.

Still, they'd had a good time. He did tease on the rare occasion. She sensed it was something inherent to his nature that had been buried beneath a learned wariness. For all that he'd come from a loving family, Max Murdock had an aloofness about him that was designed to keep people at arm's length. Zoe wasn't sure how much of it was a hazard of his former occupation and how much of it had been erected since his wife left.

Whether it could be torn down was anyone's guess.

Max and Annabelle were back home by two, but it seemed their day had just begun. After he put her down for her afternoon nap, he finished the last bit of unpacking and putting things away. Then he organized his work area so he could start back on the book the first thing on Monday morning. All in all, he was pleased with the way the cabin looked. He knew it wouldn't suit him forever, but for now, it brought him a sense of belonging he hadn't experienced in a long time.

His mom claimed she could walk into a house and tell if it was a happy house or a sad house. This one, she'd proclaimed to be happy. As silly as the premise was, Max felt it, too. Even Annabelle, whom he'd expected to have a hard time settling in, had surprised him. She toddled all through the house, exploring each room and seeming to find pleasure in her new surroundings. When he put her down for her nap, she grabbed Danny's skinny rabbit and went right to sleep.

When she awakened, he set up her playpen outside and set to work pulling weeds from the front flower beds. While he worked, Annabelle played beneath the shade of the oak tree and watched the squirrels and birds scampering and flitting around her. After a couple of hours weeding and raking, he fired up his Holland Grill, threw on a potato to bake and, later, a ribeye, which he had with another salad made from Zoe's fresh lettuce. Annabelle had something nasty-looking from a jar that was supposed to be beef stew. Despite its looks, she ate it as if it were as tasty as his steak. After dinner, he gave her a bath and put her to bed for the night. Again, she went out like a light. Nothing like good country air, he thought smiling at the picture of innocence she portrayed with the bunny hugged tightly to her.

Though Max hoped for the same, he couldn't sleep for thinking about the day. Going to Chris's game had been an unexpected pleasure. He'd been surprised at the pride he'd felt every time Chris made a good play. Being with Zoe and the boys had been nice, too. Relaxing, somehow, even though Zoe was a yeller, telling Chris, "Come on baby, you can hit it...Watch it out of his hand...choke up on your bat a little..." She knew her baseball, Max thought, and she was obviously proud of her boys' talents. It had been a good day, despite the coach's wrong assumption and the mixed pride and fear it had triggered.

Though he did it reluctantly, he also admitted it was a pleasant experience to be regarded as part of Zoe's family. Cara had never liked the things he did, so the events they attended together didn't go any farther than the occasional office party. Her office party. He'd hardly felt like a couple, much less a family. Today had been different. As terrified as he'd felt when the coach mistook him for Chris's dad, he couldn't deny a feeling of completeness as he'd sat along the fence with the kids and Zoe, knowing the other people in attendance assumed he and Zoe were the parents of her boys and Annabelle. Knowing they thought Zoe was his wife. And despite his dogged determination not to get any more involved, strangely proud of it.

Chapter Seven

Over the next three weeks, Max's life fell into a routine that was easy and pleasant, one he took no time at all adjusting to. He woke in the morning, got Annabelle up and ready and took her to Zoe's about eight. He stopped for lunch, called to check on his daughter and went back to work until five or so. On the days he was really into the story, he worked until six or six-thirty, but Zoe never complained. Some evenings, she gave him leftovers for his dinner; on a couple of occasions, she invited him to eat with her and the boys.

Annabelle had never seemed happier. When Max got her ready in the mornings and asked if she wanted to go see Zoe, she got so excited he could hardly handle her. The book was coming along nicely. Despite the time he spent staring out the window at the antics of the squirrels and birds, he might even finish it a little ahead of schedule. Life was good.

There had been a few interruptions from the boys, but they'd been pretty respectful of his work time, and Max was sure Zoe had no idea they'd slipped away to come visit. As promised, he'd fixed Mike's bicycle chain. Then the pedal had fallen off. Chris had stopped by one evening when he'd gotten home from school to see if Max wanted to go fishing with them in the creek. He'd declined and spent the rest of the afternoon wondering what the boys were doing, if they were having fun, if they were catching anything. His productivity had been so low that afternoon he might as well have gone. Most recently, Danny had asked him to go to school with him for a day honoring fathers.

"Could you come and have lunch at my school with me?" he'd pleaded, his blue eyes wide. "I'm the only kid in my class who doesn't have a dad, and I'm gonna feel real stupid sitting in the lunchroom all by myself. We're makin' you guys something, too."

Max's heart ached with sympathy. He hadn't given much thought to the many specific things fathers were expected to do with their kids. He imagined Annabelle growing up, needing—or at least hoping—he would show up for her dance recitals, or school plays, or Dad's Day. He was beginning to understand how much more there was to parenting than just providing a child with their day-to-day physical needs. He was fast learning that those were unimportant compared to their emotional and psychological requirements.

He imagined Danny's discomfiture if he were alone that day, imagined how sad he'd be, thinking of the father he'd lost who could no longer share these special times with him. And, as he sat in front of the computer and tried to write the next scene in his book, he imagined how he'd feel knowing the agony Danny was going through. So, instead of telling him the day of the father's program was a work day, he'd heard himself saying, "Sure, Danny. I'd be proud to come."

And that's how easy it was to fall into a pattern he'd never expected. That's how easy it was for the boys to entice him into sharing portions of their lives.

Zoe was another matter altogether. Unlike the boys, she never disturbed him when he was working. Her requests—all innocent—came when he took Annabelle in the mornings or picked her up in the evenings. The boys had pushed the screen door so wide, they'd ruined the old-fashioned spring. Did he have time to replace it before he left? Did he mind? The light switch in the living room wasn't working. Did he know anything about electricity? The toilet in her bathroom kept running. Did he know how to stop it?

Of course, Max knew just enough about all those things to be of help, and even though each job had set him back a half hour or more, he'd been glad to do them. Fixing her toilet had been the hardest. Not the job itself, but spending time in her most personal space. Her bedroom was light and airy, with creamy off-white walls and lacy curtains hanging in front of tall windows. Old-fashioned prints graced the walls and a huge Australian tree fern sat next to the French doors that led to the back porch. A sitting area near the fireplace boasted two wingback chairs in sage tone-on-tone damask. Her bedspread was a patchwork quilt sewn from satin and lace scraps and other decorative items in creamy whites, soft sage greens and pastel pink. The room was cheerful, classy and one hundred percent feminine.

The style of the bathroom echoed the bedroom. There, she had painted an old ladder a pure, pristine white and hung a selection of new and vintage towels on the crosspieces. An old dressing table, also painted white, sat in front of an oval mirror, and several bottles of cologne resided on a mirrored tray. A variety of makeup items were piled in a basket near a couple of bottles of sunscreen and small bottle of goat's milk hand lotion. A few hair clips were scattered atop the surface of the dresser along with an antique silver brush set. A mannequin hand attached to a piece of wood held several necklaces and chains, and a vintage hat adorned with feathers and crushed velvet roses sat atop a hat stand next to it. A fluffy white towel hung on a brass hook, and a floral gown of something thin, floral and silky lay haphazardly across the back of a chair.

The rooms, with their diverse decorating styles, were visual proof that Zoe was a complex individual, something he was beginning to see the better he became acquainted with her. She was a thoroughly modern woman with old-fashioned sentiment. The decor was also a reminder that even though she didn't mind the hard work that went hand in hand with the lifestyle she'd chosen—the gardening and canning and all the yard work—she was nevertheless all woman, with all the basic ingrained feminine needs, as the sunscreen and hand lotion affirmed.

As much as he hated to admit it, she was filling more and more of his thoughts. The situation with her and the boys wasn't to his liking—he was far from ready to get serious over her or any woman. His only defense was to try to keep them at arm's length as much as possible and to convince himself that his feelings for her were as natural to a single, long-celibate man as breathing.

In theory, his reasoning was sound. But sometimes, when he couldn't go to sleep, he'd stare out his bedroom window at her house and see the light on in her room. He wondered if she had trouble sleeping, wondered if she was as lonely as he was and if she ever thought of him the way he thought of her. And he wondered if she ever felt the same hunger to feel a warm and willing body next to hers that assaulted him when he least expected it. His thoughts, when he let down his guard, were both tantalizing and frightening.

He'd heard stories about people who'd become involved with someone else too soon after a breakup and within months had found themselves in another impossible situation. After Cara, that was the last thing he wanted or needed. The next time he became involved with a woman he wanted to be sure it was forever. A woman with three children and a mongrel dog certainly weren't in his plans for the future....

On Thursday, Max had just finished his required pages when the phone rang. When he glanced at the caller ID he saw the call was from mother.

"Hey, Mom. What's up?"

"Nothing much. I just need a small favor."

"I don't like that tone I hear in your voice," Max told her. "What kind of favor?"

"Danielle is in town for a couple of days and Paul wondered if you'd go to dinner with us in Little Rock tomorrow evening. He feels like we should do something to entertain her."

Danielle was Paul's sister's daughter. Max remembered her from his youth, when she and her family came to visit. She was pretty and he recalled that Ryan had been sweet on her at one time when they were in their teens, after it dawned on him that they weren't really related. Was his mother attempting a setup after all these years? "You and Paul aren't trying to pull a fast one, are you? "

"Of course not. You can consider it a date if you like, but really, the two of you would just be having dinner with me and Paul. Danielle went through a divorce herself a couple of years ago, so she might be a good one to talk to. I'm not asking you to marry her," Donna said. "Just come with us to dinner."

Just dinner. It didn't sound as if it would be too taxing. And it wasn't exactly as if he were getting a pig in a poke. He knew Danielle. It would probably be a pleasant evening, and there was no use kidding himself. He needed to prove that this…infatuation he had with Zoe was just that. Needed to prove that the things she made him feel could be aroused by any red-blooded woman. Danielle was a looker. If anyone could arouse him, it should be her.

"Okay," he said, before he could come up with a half-dozen reasons he shouldn't go.

"You'll go?" His mother sounded surprised.

"Sure," Max said, with as much enthusiasm as he could muster. "Like you said, it's just dinner. It might be nice to do something different. I haven't had any contact with any adults but you and Zoe in months, and Danielle was always fun. Besides, it's time I started getting on with my life."

"Good for you," Donna said. "Paul will be thrilled.

Why don't you meet us here at the house about six-thirty?"

"Sounds like a plan," Max said. "See you then."

Max walked along the path that led to Zoe's, wishing he hadn't agreed to go with his parents and Danielle. Chris, Mike and Danny saw him when he stepped from the wooded area into the edge of the yard and came running up to him, wearing wide grins. They skidded to a stop mere feet away, Mutt close on their heels, tongue lolling.

"Hey, Max!" they all chorused.

"Hey," Max replied, as they fell into step with him.

"When are we gonna practice my pitching?" Chris asked.

Max looked down at him. He'd hoped to get in a few more pages before dinner this evening while Annabelle played in her playpen, but he wouldn't be able to practice with Chris tomorrow as planned because of his date.

"How about after dinner this evening?" Max said. "I'll give you a call."

"That'd be great!" Chris said, smiling.

"Don't forget Dad's Day is tomorrow," Danny reminded, looking up at Max.

"I haven't forgotten," Max told him. He looked at Mike expectantly, but the child just looked back, his blue eyes calm beneath his shock of auburn hair. Mikey was a good kid, but adventurous, it seemed to Max. Though he was the middle child, he seemed like the most confident of the three, the one who'd take a double-dog dare in a heartbeat. He had the hottest temper, but it left as quickly as it came. He also seemed interested in more dangerous pursuits…like swinging on muscadine vines over the creek where he insisted on wading, even though it looked like a perfect habitation for a water moccasin. So far, Mike had been the least vocal in asking Max for things.

Now, sensing he should say something, Mike asked, "Have you ever written a book for kids?"

Of all the things he might have guessed Mike would ask, this was one subject of conversation that had never crossed Max's mind. "No, Mike, I haven't."

"Why not?"

Max stopped in his tracks. The boys did the same. Why not? Because he knew nothing about kids? Because he didn't have the slightest idea what might interest a child? "I don't know," he said. "I guess I never thought about it."

"I wish you would," Mike told him. "I'm sick of all my books. They're all baby books."

"Baby books?"

"Yeah. They got animals in them doing stupid stuff. I want a real story, with kids who act like real kids act."

"And how's that?" Max asked.

"Well, they aren't good all the time. Sometimes they disobey their mom." He looked uncomfortable for a second, then hurried to say, "They aren't bad all the time, either. Sometimes they fight with their brothers and sisters. Like me and Chris and Danny do. I want to read a story about a kid who does something. A kid who has ventures."

"Ventures?" Max asked, his brow furrowing in question. Then it hit him. "Oh! You want a kid who has adventures. Maybe your mom can find you something like that at the library."

"Nah," Mike said with a disgusted shake of his head. "We already tried. There isn't anything the librarian thought would be good for a kid my age. I'd like to read Harry Potter all by myself, but I can't read yet."

Max picked up the pace again and slanted a glance down at Mike. "What kind of adventures would you like to see?"

Mike gave a negligent shrug. "I don't know. Something like the kid in that *Raiders* movie. Maybe he's looking for a lost diamond or something." Mike looked up at Max with pleading in his eyes. "Would you, Max?"

"What?"

"Write me a book of my very own. Then if I like it, you can keep doing them."

Right. Just when did Mike think he'd do his real writing? The kind that paid real money? He paused at the back porch steps. "Tell you what, Mike. When I finish the book I'm writing right now, I'll think about writing you a story. I just don't know if I can write a book a kid would like or not. And I have to do my other book first, because that's how I make money to pay my bills."

Mike thought about that for a moment. "Okay. But just think about it, like you said."

"Da da." The sound of Annabelle's voice drew his gaze from Mike to the back door, where Annabelle stood, her pudgy hands pressed to the screen, her nose flattened against the wire mesh, smiling in pleasure at the group of males at the bottom of the steps.

"Hey, baby girl," Max said, starting toward her.

"Her nose is gonna look like a waffle," Mike said, as the trio of Barlow boys followed.

"Yeah," Danny agreed. "It's gonna have little squares all over."

Max squatted down to Annabelle's level and pressed his right hand against hers. "Hi."

"Hi!" she said, smiling.

More progress every day he thought. "Where's Zoe?"

As if she understood the question, Annabelle rattled off some sort of answer he couldn't begin to understand.

"I'm coming!" Zoe called from the dimness of the hallway. She scooped Annabelle up into her arms and unlocked the screen door, pushing it wide open. "We were waiting for you, and the phone rang. Annabelle saw you coming, and she was so excited I didn't have the heart to drag her away. I grabbed the phone and came right back."

"You don't have to explain why she was here alone," Max told her, meeting her anxious gaze with his own. "I know you're taking good care of her, and I know you don't leave her unattended if you think she'll get hurt. I also know that kids can get hurt even when there is an adult around."

"Max is gonna work on my pitching after supper," Chris said. "So can we eat as soon as he leaves?"

"Here's your hat. What's your hurry?" Zoe said to Max with a grin, quoting one of her grandmother's favorite sayings.

"He said he hadn't forgotten about Dad's Day at school tomorrow," Danny chimed in.

"I didn't suppose he had," Zoe told him, ruffling his hair.

"He's gonna write me a book of my very own," Mike told her.

"He said he'd think about it, dodo," Chris said. "*After* he gets finished with his real book."

"Mine's gonna be a real book," Mike argued. "It's just not gonna be as fat."

"Whoa!" Zoe said. "Stop arguing, you two." She handed Annabelle, who was reaching for Max, over to him. "Did you actually say you'd write him a book?"

"I did say I'd think about it," Max corrected, brushing his nose against Annabelle's. "I have no earthly idea how to write a story for kids."

"Anything but baby stuff," Zoe told him with an arched eyebrow. "It's all I hear. Especially now that I'm reading to Annabelle and he and Danny are sitting in."

"Is it baby stuff?"

"Definitely," Zoe said. "You boys go on and play while I get Annabelle's things together," she told them. "Then you can walk Max to the edge of the woods when they go home."

Grumbling, they nonetheless went on their way. Max followed Zoe to the den and stopped in his tracks when he saw what was hanging over the mantel. The portrait of David. Seeing the genial, smiling face looking down at him, Max was stunned to feel a sharp pang of something explode inside him. He was even more surprised when he realized it was jealousy. Striving to keep his voice even and nonconfrontational—why should he feel so fighting mad?—he said, "I see you hung the painting."

"Yeah," she said, turning with a smile. "It seemed a shame not to. The boys are forgetting him to some degree, I think. And Danny doesn't remember him at all. I don't want them dwelling on the past, but I don't want them to forget David, either. I thought the portrait might help them to remember."

"It can't hurt," Max heard himself say. "You must have loved him very much."

Her smile was fleeting, a little sad. "How did you know?"

"There's love in every brush stroke," Max told her truthfully.

"David saved me from myself," she told him, thrusting one of Annabelle's toys into the bag.

"Meaning?"

"Meaning that in my youth I had a tendency to fall for the wrong kind of guy. I was drawn to them like a magnet."

"What kind of guy is that?" Max asked, unable to squelch his curiosity.

"The kind more interested in himself than me. The kind who claimed to love me, but would never make the commitment. The kind who walked on me, used me and cheated on me."

"I find that hard to believe," Max told her, surprised by the statement. "If ever there was a person secure in who she is, it's you."

"Now. Thanks to David."

"And what did the miracle worker do?"

Zoe's eyebrows drew together in a frown. "You say that mockingly," she said in a quiet voice. "Why?"

Realizing that he'd let his jealousy show, Max said. "Sorry. It's just hard for me to believe that one person can change another that much."

"Don't you know? Love is a miracle cure, Max," Zoe said. "And it heals all sorts of things—emotional things."

"And David healed you by loving you?"

She nodded.

"What did he heal you of?"

"A lack of self-worth." She lifted her chin a little, almost defiantly, he thought. "My mother and dad divorced when I was seven. My mother remarried when I was ten. My stepfather had custody of his two daughters, who were nothing less than stunningly beautiful. They also happened to be clever and popular. Not to mention spoiled brats." The last was said with a bright smile. "I grew up a victim of the Cinderella syndrome."

"Complete with wicked stepsisters."

"Not wicked. Spoiled. They were the ones who got most of the new things. I got the hand-me-downs. Mom wasn't strong enough to stand up for me, so..." Her voice trailed away, the words speaking for themselves.

"They got the cream of the crop. You got the leftovers."

"Right." She smiled suddenly. "I was smarter than they were, though. And more talented. I was the one who excelled at art and brought home the A's. As I got older, I began to see that Mom had divorced dad and married someone twice as bad. At least Dad didn't run around on her the way Calvin did. They say you marry someone like your parents, so I was on a headlong course of emotional self-destruction, falling for the same type of guy Mom had."

"And then you met David."

"And then I met David. He was funny and smart and very much aware of who he was, where he'd come from and where he was headed. He made me take a long hard look at my past and where I was, and helped me to see the pattern in my choices. Thank God I found him. He was a wonderful father and husband."

"Hard to replace."

"He could never be replaced," she said honestly. "I may meet someone else I'll love just as much, but it will be a different love because he'll be a different person."

Neither spoke for several seconds. Struggling with what she'd told him, the silence grew longer. Finally, she broke the awkward stillness by asking, "What about you?"

"What about me?" Max asked, glancing at her questioningly.

"I've told you all about me. It's your turn. What happened to your marriage?"

Max didn't reply for several seconds. "Looking back, I think maybe I was the kind of guy you were talking about. I was on the Little Rock police force, and I loved it. It's a hard life for wives, I'm told, always worrying, never sure whether or not their mate will come through the door or if they'll see his body being loaded into an ambulance on the five o'clock news."

Now that he'd admitted that much, it seemed easier to go on. "Cara hated it from the first day of our marriage. She was always begging me to quit and, selfishly, I wouldn't, because I loved it, and it was all I knew how to do."

"I wouldn't call that selfish," Zoe told him, sitting down on the wide arm of the sofa. "I'd call that dedicated."

"Maybe," he conceded with a shrug.

"What kind of work did she do?"

Max pushed a lock of curly hair away from Annabelle's face. "Real estate. She was darn good at it. Anyway, the longer we were married, the worse things got. I got wounded during a drug bust, which gave her more ammunition to use against me. By this time, I'd been playing with the writing for a couple of years and was getting some good feedback. While I was still in therapy, I heard a publisher wanted a book I'd sent, so I gave in to Cara and quit the force, even though I wasn't sure it was the right thing to do. It didn't help the marriage much. I think by then, it was too far gone."

"It happens that way sometimes," Zoe said.

"Strangely, she got pregnant right after I quit the force. She wasn't too thrilled about the idea of motherhood, but she decided to have the baby—thank God." He smiled at Annabelle, a smile that said just how thankful he was.

"I don't mean to be judgmental," Zoe told him, "but I can't imagine anyone not being thrilled about having a child."

"Cara is a very beautiful woman. She didn't like the changes motherhood made to her body, either during or after the pregnancy. In some ways, she seemed to resent Annabelle, even though I have to admit she did a good job taking care of her. Or at least I thought she did."

"Why did she leave? You did tell me she left you?"

He nodded. "I came home from my therapy session one day and she was gone. She left a note saying she'd left Annabelle with a neighbor and that it had all been a mistake. The whole five years we were together."

Max wasn't sure, but he thought he saw the glimmer of tears in Zoe's eyes. "I'm so sorry."

"Yeah," he said. "Me, too. I always thought that outside of death, marriage was forever. Naive of me, huh?"

"No. Just a way of thinking that's gone out of style. We're a throwaway society. We've been conditioned that if it breaks, or isn't what we expected, or we get tired of it, we trade it in, take it back or get rid of it. Commitment is a word that few people today have any conception of, and if they do understand it, they seldom practice it."

"I agree."

"So you were left with Annabelle, and you had no idea what to do?"

"Right. I had another book to write, but I couldn't do that and watch the baby. My mom kept her for a while, but when I contacted you, she'd told me that she and my stepdad wanted to do some traveling. I panicked. I didn't want to leave her with just anyone. I was really glad to find you." He smiled. "Despite our bad beginning."

"Thanks," she said, smiling back. "I've thoroughly enjoyed Annabelle, and the boys adore her."

"The feeling's mutual, I think."

"And you're getting better with her, even the short time you've been here. You don't have that look of terror in your eyes when you deal with her that I saw when we first met."

"It was that noticeable?"

"Yep," she said with a lift of her eyebrows. "Pretty bad."

"She scared me to death when she was so small," he admitted. "I'd never been around babies before, and I had no idea what to do for her or to her. But now that she's getting older, she doesn't seem quite so fragile. And she's communicating some, too, and that helps."

"It does," Zoe agreed.

"Having the boys around has been wonderful for us both. They've given me a better perspective on the whole kid thing. You've done a good job with them, Zoe. They're great kids."

Another of those silences stretched between them. Max reached out and picked up a container of wipes. As he did, he turned toward a far wall. He couldn't hide his surprise at what he saw. An easel with a stretched canvas sat near a window with a northern exposure. He was even more surprised to see that the subject of the painting was, from all indications, his daughter.

"You're painting Annabelle?" he asked, going over to the picture.

Zoe looked embarrassed. "I meant to hide it before you came."

"Why?"

"I don't know if I have what it takes to paint anymore. It's been so long."

"What made you decide to try?"

She shrugged self-consciously. "The things you and Paul said that night, I guess. You made me remember how much I used to love the creative process and gave me hope that I might find some pleasure in it again." She laughed. "Looking back, it's hard to believe I gave it up. It would probably have been great therapy when David died."

"Why Annabelle?" he asked, glancing again at the rough sketch of his daughter.

"Why not?" Zoe countered, cramming the skinny rabbit into Annabelle's bag. "She's beautiful."

"That she is," he said. "I'll be happy to pay you for the portrait when you're finished."

Zoe handed him the cloth bag. "Oh, no!" she said. "I'm not doing it for money. It's for practice. It may be terrible."

"It may be a masterpiece."

"Of course, there's always that possibility," she said,

tongue in cheek. She smiled at the baby. "Bye, sweet thing. See you tomorrow."

She stepped nearer and leaned in to kiss Annabelle on the cheek. Close enough that her head brushed his chin. Close enough that he could smell the subtle scent of roses. He drew in a sharp breath and Zoe's head jerked back sharply. Their eyes met—his gaze probing, hers questioning, asking questions neither had answers for. As he watched, her tongue came out and skimmed her lips, as if they'd gone dry suddenly. If they were, they weren't now. Now they were wet and tempting, full and shapely, begging to be kissed. And he wanted to kiss them. Wanted it more than he remembered ever wanting to kiss a woman.

His head lowered imperceptibly, giving her ample opportunity to stop him, giving him time to gauge her reaction, prolonging the anticipation growing inside him. Amazingly, she didn't back away. He could hear the soft sighing of her slow, measured breathing and was peripherally aware of the rise and fall of her breasts.

His head lowered more, until their mouths were mere inches apart. He felt her breath now, smelled the hint of spearmint. "Zoe." Her name was little more than an exhalation of his own breath. Plea. Supplication. Benediction.

Regrettably, as soft as it was, the sound of his voice broke the spell binding them.

As if she suddenly realized she was about to step off into the deep end of the pool with only minimal swimming skills, she drew in a sharp little gasp and took an involuntary step back. She gave a shake of her head, as if to reject what had just happened between them, or perhaps to dislodge any lingering, unacceptable emotions.

She started to turn away, but Max reached out his free hand and grasped her upper arm. Her gaze flew to his once again. There was surprise in her eyes. Maybe even disbelief. Her gaze lowered from his to his hand on her arm. It was the first time he'd touched her. Her skin was as silky soft as he'd imagined, as he'd known it would be from his dreams. Soft and warm.

"Wait."

She looked at him, curiosity now filling her eyes.

He released his hold on her arm and immediately realized how much he missed just touching a woman. "I'm sorry."

"For what?" she asked, but they both knew what he was talking about. Before he could put it into words, she shook her head again. "Forget it. It's no big thing."

No big thing? Max thought incredulously. Maybe not to her, but his blood pressure was still sky-high. He saw that her cheeks were flushed and there was an unnatural brightness in her eyes. Maybe she wasn't as indifferent as she let on.

"I don't want to keep you," she said, as if she'd held him up in some way. "You have to get your dinner, so you can help Chris later. I'll see you tomorrow."

It was as cool a dismissal as he'd ever received. He knew she was doing her best to salvage the moment, knew she was trying to put things back to a normal footing. Knew it was best that they maintain the status quo.

"Yeah," he said, hoping he didn't sound as dazed as he felt. "Tomorrow." He paused, searching his mind for the fragment of information the word triggered. Something he needed to tell her. Then it hit him. Dinner with Danielle.

"Oh, I, uh, wanted to ask if you'd mind keeping Annabelle for me tomorrow night." He might have imagined it, but he thought he saw a question flash briefly in her blue eyes. "Paul's niece is coming to town for a few days and they want me to go with them to Little Rock for dinner. Make a foursome. It's not a date or anything—" why had he said that? "—but we probably won't be back until late. It would make a long day for you."

"Of course, I'll keep her. I'm having a friend over for dinner, but one more won't be a problem."

Max's mind ran wild. Was her friend male or female?

When he didn't say anything, she said, "It's no problem, Max. Really," she said. "Jack won't mind."

Jack. A man. So she dates, he thought. What had given him the idea that she didn't? She'd been a widow for three years. There was no reason to believe that during that time she hadn't had the occasional casual date. It was casual, he assumed. Hoped. Damn! What was the matter with him? He was like the legendary dog in the manger. Convinced he didn't want her himself, but not wanting anyone else to have her, either.

"No way." He was surprised at the firmness in his voice. "I'm not going to wreck your one night of fun by having you baby-sit my daughter."

"This isn't a date, if that's what you're thinking," she told him. "Jack is just a friend going through a divorce."

Yeah, right. Which meant Jack was lonely, no doubt looking for a feminine shoulder to cry on…and a place to lay his head.

"That's okay," he said, seething with sudden, irrational jealousy. "I'll call Julie and see if she can watch her."

"I really don't mind," Zoe said. "Are you sure?"

"Positive." Max grabbed Annabelle's bag, turned and headed for the back door. Somehow, he managed to dodge the boys as he made his way across the yard. His mind was roiling with the depth of his animosity, as well as the kiss that had almost transpired between him and Zoe. He wondered what it would have been like to feel her lips beneath his and how he was going to survive if he didn't find out soon. And he wondered if this Jack person would know before his evening with Zoe was over.

Chapter Eight

As soon as Max left, Zoe began to pace the room. She had to think this through, try to get some perspective on what had just happened. She could tell herself that he hadn't kissed her, so nothing had really happened, but that would be a lie. Whether or not their lips touched, they had crossed some invisible line in their relationship, and it had begun the moment they trusted each other enough to share the heartbreak of their pasts. They had moved beyond a casual relationship to something more personal, but what? Attraction, for sure. Understanding each other, definitely. What about caring? She liked him, of course, cared for him as a person, as a new friend, even.

If that's all it is, why are you so jealous? Jealous? Is that what this feeling was? It had been years since she'd experienced the emotion. Jealousy was something she'd never had to deal with during her years with David. He'd never given her a reason to feel it. Yet the fact remained that Max was going on a date, and she didn't like the idea one bit.

Stunned by this new development, Zoe felt tears prickling beneath her eyelids. Granted, Max's date was a relative of sorts, but they weren't *really* related, which meant he *might* look at her as an available, attractive woman. *She's probably gorgeous. The kind to knock a man's socks off. Or his pants.* Zoe pressed her hands to her hot cheeks and shook her head. Good grief! Where had that come from? Where was any of this coming from? She couldn't be jealous. She hardly knew the man.

Maybe so, but if your reaction to him a few minutes ago is anything to go by, that's something that you obviously want to change.

"No."

Even as the word of denial echoed throughout the emptiness of the room, she knew it was a lie. She wanted nothing more than to see what it felt like to have those lips moving over hers. She wouldn't be happy until she felt his arms around her and experienced the touch of his body pressed against hers. And heaven help her, she wouldn't be satisfied until she felt what it was like to be possessed by him, body, heart and soul. To be loved by him.

Love? She gave a little cry of despair. The thought that she could be falling in love with Max frightened her more than the idea of living alone without David. Not the notion of love itself. She'd always hoped she would find another man to spend the rest of her life with. But falling in love with a man like Max wasn't in her plans. Max was entirely too much like the men she'd fallen for in the past…before David.

No, that wasn't true. Max wasn't a self-centered, selfish man, but neither was he a sharing sort of man. He wouldn't come home at the end of his day and tell her what was bothering him. He wasn't the kind of man to talk things through or disclose his hopes, dreams or fears. He would guard his hopes, fearing they wouldn't materialize. He would watch out for his dreams, certain something might happen to keep them from coming true. And he would deny his fears, feeling they might be a sign of weakness. Weakness of any kind— real or imagined—was poison to a man like Max Murdock.

On the plus side, he was strong and dependable, the kind of man who would be there for you in any tough situation. He was dedicated and talented, as his writing proved. He might even be changing, since he'd gotten a new career and a baby to care for. Whether or not he realized it, he had a softer side, and she had seen definite changes in his attitudes in the scant month he'd been living at the cabin. His patience with the boys and his willingness to help them confirmed that. The big question was, had he changed—could he change— enough to be the kind of husband she needed and wanted, the kind of man who would be a good parent to her sons? The sound of the screen door slamming shut brought Zoe back to reality.

Was she insane? Why on earth would she even think of Max and marriage in the same breath? Her question was immaterial, since the real question had nothing to do with how Max would shape up as a husband and father. The real question was why would a man like him want to tie himself to a woman with three kids when he could have any woman he wanted?

"Mom, is supper ready yet?" Chris asked, coming to a halt in the den doorway. "I want to get as much pitching practice in with Max as I can before dark."

"We're just having sandwiches. It won't take long," Zoe assured him, heading for the kitchen. Max. Her whole world was beginning to revolve around him, and that wasn't good.

Forty-five minutes later, the dishwasher was loaded, the laundry was folded, and there was nothing for Zoe to do except watch out the kitchen window as Max and Chris practiced pitching. The dog was chasing something in the woods near Annabelle's playpen, which Max had set up beneath the widespread boughs of a black gum tree. Mike and Danny seemed to be dividing their time between playing with Annabelle and cavorting with the dog.

Zoe watched as Chris, who was standing on a mound of dirt Max had built up for him, threw a ball to Max, who was in a crouching position several yards away. She heard the ball smack into Max's worn catcher's mitt, probably the one he'd used in college. He lobbed the ball back to Chris, who caught it easily.

Mutt raced across the yard to the mound. Chris tried to get him to go away, but the dog thought Chris was playing and waited for him to throw the ball for him to fetch, his tail wagging ninety to nothing. Mike and Danny got into the fray, and before long, chaos had broken loose. Max rose from his squatting position and headed that way, an expression of irritation on his rugged face.

It was time for good ol' mom to come to the rescue, Zoe thought with a sigh. She both wanted to see Max and dreaded it. How would he react to her after their near kiss? She drew in a deep breath and wiped suddenly sweaty palms down the sides of her shorts. Only one way to find out.

She stepped out onto the porch and stood at the top of the steps, gripping the post. Chris was on the ground, Mutt, who was growing into a monster of a dog, was on top of him, licking his face, while Mike and Danny pulled on his collar. Max stood watching, the irritation replaced with a smile of pleasure.

Seeing her standing there, Mike called, "Come get this dang dog, Mom. Chris can't even practice."

"Coming!" Zoe called, starting down the steps. Mike's words had galvanized Max into action. As she crossed the lawn, she saw him cross the few yards separating him from the boys, grab the dog's collar and pull him off Chris. She kept her gaze focused on the boys, knowing Max's watchful eyes were on her. She felt awkward, self-conscious, as gauche as a teenager with her first crush. As she neared the group, she saw Chris get to his feet and scrub at his face with the tail of his T-shirt.

"I'll take the dog," she said, reaching out to take hold of the leather collar. As she did, her hand encountered the warmth of Max's, and she looked up at him. The expression in his eyes was intense, watchful, as if he, too, were trying to gauge how she was going to behave with him. It was one of the more awkward moments of her life. She wasn't sure when she'd been so aware of herself as a woman, so aware of a man. She didn't remember ever feeling so uncertain about what to do or say. It was only when Max released his hold on the collar that she found her voice.

"How's he doing?" she asked. She was dimly aware that Annabelle, who had suddenly realized she was no longer the center of attraction, had begun to cry, vaguely aware that all three of the boys raced to the playpen, eager to placate her.

Max frowned. "Who, Mutt?"

"Chris," Zoe said with a shake of her head.

The look in Max's eyes cleared suddenly. "Oh. He's doing great. Getting a lot more speed and accuracy."

"You'll watch that he doesn't do too much, won't you?" she asked, a frown puckering her forehead. "I don't want him ruining his arm at the age of ten."

"I won't let him hurt himself," Max promised.

"Thanks." Neither of them spoke for a few seconds. Finally, Zoe asked, "Is Julie watching Annabelle tomorrow night?"

"Yeah," he said, nodding. "In fact, Celia told me to bring the playpen, and they'd keep her overnight, since I'd probably be late getting home."

"Oh," Zoe said. "Good idea." Mutt lunged, trying to get away. "I've got to go tie this dog up before he jerks my arm out of socket." Clutching the dog's collar, Zoe turned to walk away.

"Zoe!"

She turned.

"What time should I leave for the Dad's Day bash in the morning?"

"Danny's lunch is at eleven, and I think the dads were supposed to take a look at some things in the classroom first, so I'd say you should get there by ten-fifteen or so."

"I'll be there."

Suddenly, and for no reason she could imagine, Zoe felt her throat tighten and tears sting beneath her eyelids. Her uncertainty and embarrassment fled before a more meaningful emotion. "I really appreciate your doing this for Danny, Max."

"I'm glad to go."

"Well, it means a lot to him, and me. Sometimes, I think he's the one who misses having a dad the most. Not that Chris and Mike don't miss him," she hastened to add.

"All kids need a father," Max said. "I think they all need two parents, no matter how good a job one may do. It's something about balance. Men and women view things differently, react to situations differently, and I think it's good and healthy for a child to see both ways."

Zoe smiled. "That's pretty profound for a man who confessed an hour or so ago that he was scared to death of his daughter."

Max smiled back and Zoe's heart took its customary nosedive. "Just because I understand how things should be, doesn't mean I'm able to do it."

"Like I said, I think you've come a long way. Being Annabelle's dad won't ever be easy, but it will get easier, if that makes any sense."

"About as much sense as any of it does," he told her. Another of those unexpected, familiar silences hung between them. Max cleared his throat and said, "Look, about what happened earlier..."

"Nothing happened earlier," she said quickly, tugging on the dog's collar to make him sit.

"Whether or not I kissed you, something happened, and you know it."

"It was just the moment," she said with a shrug.

"Was it?" he challenged. When she didn't answer, he said, "Look, I'm not going to insult your intelligence by denying that I'm attracted to you. I am."

Zoe's heart skipped a beat at the admission. The dog yanked at her, eager to be free. "Stop it!" she said, sharply.

Max looked stunned. "I beg your pardon?"

"Not you," she said. "The dog."

"Oh." He looked confused, as if he'd lost his train of thought. "But I have to say that attracted to you or not, it's only fair to tell you that I'm too close to my divorce to be ready for another relationship just now."

Zoe raised her chin to a defiant level. "Oh!" she said, striving for nonchalance. "I hope I haven't led you to believe that I'm looking for one, though I can't deny that you're an attractive man. I think it's just…that we have so much close contact…um…with the kids and everything."

"Right," he said with a nod. "I agree. Anyway, I wanted to clear the air. We don't need any kind of tension between us."

"No," she said. "We have to spend too much time together for that."

"Right." He gave her a smile that looked half-embarrassed, half-relieved.

"Hey Max!" Chris yelled. "When are we gonna start practicin' again?"

Max dragged his gaze from Zoe's and turned to Chris. "Be there in just a minute," he called.

"Hey, Max!" Mike called. "Annabelle's got a dirty diaper."

Zoe saw a look of dismay cross his face. "I'll change

her as soon as I tie up the dog. That way, you can get on with the practice."

"You're an angel," he said.

"Sure," she said with a wry smile. "Just let me go tie up Mutt." She turned away and headed for the dog's chain, thinking that for two people who'd cleared the air so there wouldn't be any tension between them, the conversation was definitely stilted. She also thought that for a woman who prided herself on her honesty, she'd just lied through her teeth. She'd had no choice. There was no way she could admit to Max that not only was she attracted to him, she thought that first attraction was somehow, against her better judgment, growing into something more.

The next morning, Max waited to take Annabelle to Zoe's until he left for the elementary school. Maybe it was because he was in a hurry and didn't notice, or maybe the awkwardness had really passed, but Zoe seemed fine. She looked fine, too. All scrubbed and sweet, her auburn hair pulled up into a jaunty ponytail. Barefoot, she was wearing a pair of denim shorts that left her long freckle-dusted legs bare and a sage-green cotton sleeveless shirt tied at her midriff.

She took Annabelle from him and gave her a kiss on the cheek. "Hey, precious girl," she said. "How are you this morning?" Annabelle mumbled something, and Zoe said, "Good, are you? So am I." She turned to Max. "How about you?"

"I'm good, too," Max said, setting the diaper bag on the countertop. He rotated his arm at the shoulder. "A little sore from tossing the ball around yesterday. That's pretty sad. I guess I'm getting a little creaky in my old age," he joked.

She smiled. "That's what I think every time I work in the garden."

Max saw her gaze drift over him from head to toe. "You look very nice."

"I wasn't sure what to wear."

"The khakis are good, and the burgundy shirt is a good color for you."

"I'm glad you approve," he told her. He glanced at his watch. "I'd better get a move on. I don't want to be late and have Danny worrying about where I am. Do you have any idea how long it will last?"

"I think you just look around the room at what they've done, some springtime decorations or something, and then you go to lunch. You can leave after that."

"Good," he said, nodding. "I need to try to get a few more pages done before I leave for dinner." As soon as the words left his mouth, he wished he could call them back. The sparkle vanished from Zoe's eyes, and he could almost feel the distance she was putting between them. Knowing that whatever he said would only aggravate the situation, he said, "I'd better go. See you tomorrow."

Zoe watched him leave, her heart aching. She didn't want to think of him out with another woman, but there was nothing she could do about it. "What's wrong with me, Annabelle? Why do I do this to myself? And why do I feel this way toward him when I know he's nothing but a heartbreaker?"

Annabelle smiled and, as if she sensed Zoe needed some comfort, she leaned forward and planted a wet, open-mouthed kiss on her cheek. Zoe blinked back tears. "Thanks, sweetie," she told the baby, kissing her back. "No offense, but I wish that had come from your dad."

As Max pulled into the school parking lot, he did his best to push aside the memory of the way he'd left Zoe and tried to concentrate on his upcoming time with Danny. He needed to be upbeat and positive, not down, the way he really felt. Taking a deep breath, he stepped through the doors of the elementary school and was assaulted immediately with the scent of yeast rolls, fried chicken and a rush of forgotten memories of his own childhood. The library where he'd read every biography and every Hardy Boys mystery. The cafeteria where he'd hidden his green peas beneath his mashed potatoes because they had to at least "taste" everything. Mrs. Herrington, his fifth grade teacher who looked like an angel with her blond hair and blue eyes. He'd been in love with her the entire year, until Molly Madison moved to town and stole his heart away. Max smiled at the memories, things he hadn't thought of in decades. What a shame that living life robbed a person of the time it took to take out recollections and let them play through your mind on occasion. It was only when something unexpected triggered them that they returned in all their nostalgic sweetness.

A sign at the front door had stated that he was to register at the office before proceeding to the classroom, which was fine with him, since he had no idea where he was going. A pretty woman who was clearly pregnant pushed the sign-in page toward him.

"Who are you here for?" she asked.

"Danny Barlow. Preschool. Mrs. Rogers' class."

"So you're Danny's dad?" she said, smiling. "He's really a sweetheart."

"Actually," Max said, "I'm just a friend of the family. Danny's dad is dead."

"Oh, I'm sorry for the mistake," she said.

"No problem."

She handed him a visitor's badge. "Here you go, Mr.—" she glanced at the paper "—Murdock. Mrs. Rogers' room is straight down this hallway. Take the first right and it's the third door on the left."

"Thanks," Max said, offering her one of his rare smiles.

She only nodded. As he started down the hall, she said, "You'll need to turn in your badge when you leave."

"Will do," he said, sketching her a sharp salute.

Danny's room was easy to find. The teacher's name was beside the door, and there were two rows of springtime flowers cut from construction paper with each child's picture in the center. Danny's red hair was spiked, and he was smiling broadly, his blue eyes twinkling with the mischief Max had become familiar with. Even his freckles seemed lively. Max felt a tug at his heart and smiled as he rapped on the door.

A fifty-something woman opened the door wide, a welcoming smile on her face. Max stepped into the room and felt twenty-odd pairs of curious eyes fixed on him. He saw Danny give a little wave and waved back.

"Come in," the teacher said. "You're the first one here." She extended her hand. "I'm Phyllis Rogers."

"Max Murdock," he said, taking her hand in his. She had a nice firm handshake, which he liked.

Phyllis Rogers' forehead puckered in a frown. "Murdock?" she echoed, trying to place him with a student.

"I'm with Danny Barlow."

"Oh. You're Danny's stepfather."

"No," Max said for the second time in five minutes.

"Oh, but Danny said—" The teacher's voice broke off, and she nodded as if suddenly understanding. She turned where the class couldn't see what she was saying. "Danny said his stepfather was coming," she told Max in an apologetic voice.

Not sure how to reply to that, Max plunged his hands into the pockets of his khakis. "Oh."

"I see it often with children from broken homes. They want a parent so badly, they sometimes do whatever they can to have them, if only for a while."

"Danny's parents aren't divorced," Max said. "His father died three years ago."

"And you're just a friend of the family?"

"Actually, I rent a cabin on Mrs. Barlow's farm, and she keeps my baby girl while I work. I'm a single father." Max knew the teacher was trying to figure out just what kind of role he played in Danny's life. "Mrs. Barlow's boys and I have gotten pretty tight."

"That's wonderful," Mrs. Rogers said. "It's good for a child—especially boys—to have a male influence in their lives."

Another knock sounded at the door, and another father poked his head in. Mrs. Rogers motioned for the newcomer to come in. "Why don't you go on over and say hi to Danny," she told Max. "Then you can have him show you around the room at the things we've been doing the past few weeks. All the children have made their fathers a gift. I hope you'll enjoy yours."

"Thanks," Max said. "If Danny made it, I'm sure I will."

"All right, children," she said, turning to the class. "When your father arrives, you may leave your seat and show them around the room, but be a quiet as you can so we don't interrupt Mrs. McDonald's class."

Danny leaped from his seat so quickly it looked as if he'd been sitting on a spring. He made a beeline for Max and grabbed him around the legs.

"Hey, kiddo," he said, ruffling the boy's hair.

"Hi!" Danny said, beaming up at him. "I'm really glad you came."

"Me, too," Max said, smiling down at him. He glanced around the room. "Why don't you show me what you've been working on?"

"I want to give you your present first." Danny reached under his desk and handed Max a small square package wrapped in a section of the Sunday comics and tied with green yarn.

"Should I open it now?"

"Yeah. Go ahead." Danny was smiling from ear to ear.

Carefully, Max pulled off the yarn and peeled back the tape. Inside was a block of wood with a piece of carpet glued to one side. Max couldn't help smiling at the memory it resurrected. He'd made one for his father when he was in elementary school.

"Do you know what it is?" Danny asked.

"I sure do," Max told him with a smile. "It's to shine my shoes with."

"Right!" Danny said, beaming. "Do you like it?"

"I love it. I'll use it tonight before I go out to dinner."

"Cool," Danny said. Then he grabbed Max's hand and led him to a wall where samples of printed letters were framed with construction paper. "This one is mine," he said, pointing proudly to one that bore a big gold star.

"That's very good, Danny."

"Thanks, Max. I can write my whole name now. Mrs. Rogers is a real good teacher. And she's real nice, too."

"I can tell that," Max said. "What else have you done?"

Danny led Max to a table where some ribbons had been threaded through the holes in plastic strawberry containers. "These are May baskets. I made this one for Mom. On the first day of May, you're supposed to pick flowers to put in them, hang them on the door, knock and run someplace where you can see the person's face when they answer the door. Cool, huh?"

"Way cool, Danny," Max said, remembering that he and Ryan had done the same thing when they were kids.

"Do you think Mom will like it?"

"I think your mom would like anything you did for her," he said with a smile.

Danny caught Max's hand again and pulled him toward another wall. "This is the watercolor painting I did. It's supposed to be our house and our family."

"I can see that," Max said. "There's the gazebo," he said, pointing.

"Yeah," Danny said, his excitement growing. "And this is our family, even Mutt. See, there's me and Mikey and Mom. You can tell it's us 'cause we got red hair. And this is Chris. He has brown hair like Dad."

"I see." Max saw a taller, dark-haired figure with jeans standing next to Danny's likeness of his mother.

"That must be your dad," he said, his throat tightening with a sudden rush of feeling. He was vaguely aware that more fathers had arrived and that the room was filling up, growing noisier, but it seemed as if he and Danny were alone.

"No!" Danny said. "That's not Dad. He died. That's you. And that's Annabelle over in her playpen under the tree. You're part of our family since you moved to our farm."

The lump in Max's throat grew larger. For the first time since the day he found Cara's letter of farewell, he felt the burning of tears beneath his eyelids. He was humbled and honored to be the recipient of the love he knew the child standing next to him felt for him. He cleared his throat and put a hand on Danny's shoulder.

"Thank you for including me and Annabelle in your picture, but we aren't really your family, Danny." Max actually saw the happiness in Danny's eyes fade. He felt like a bully who got his kicks from pulling the wings from butterflies.

Danny dropped his head. "I feel like you're my family," he mumbled.

Max tipped his head back and looked up at the noise-quieting tiles of the ceiling. What did he say now? How did he repair what might be irreparable damage to Danny's image of himself? Before he could think of what to say, Danny said, "I have a 'fession to make, Max."

What now? Max thought. "What's that, Danny?"

Danny raised his head and met Max's gaze head-on. "I told Mrs. Rogers you were my stepfather."

"I know," Max said in a quiet voice.

"You aren't mad, are you?"

"No, Danny," Max said, with a shake of his head.

"I'm not mad. I know that your Dad was a fine man, and a good father. I'm honored that you think I could ever compare to him in any way."

"What's compare?" Danny asked.

"That you think I could be like him."

"I don't know if you're like my dad or not," Danny said. He scrunched his features up as if her were trying very hard to come up with a recollection. "I don't remember him. Sometimes I think I do, but I don't. Not really. All I know is that you act like a dad to me. And you're the only dad I've ever had."

Again, Max was left speechless, struggling to find words to express his feelings to the child who was being so open and honest with him.

"Max?"

"Yeah, Danny?"

"You could be my dad if you wanted to," he said wistfully.

"How's that?"

"Chris said that if you and mom got married, you'd be our stepfather, and Annabelle would be our sister."

"You and Chris have talked about this?"

"Yeah," he said with a vigorous nod. "Mikey, too."

"And how do the three of you feel about that?"

"We'd really like it if you would marry her, Max. We'd really like you to be our dad."

Feeling as if he were in a riptide that was pulling him farther and farther from safety and closer to tears than he had been in years, Max urged a small smile to his lips and tried to joke his way out of the serious discussion. "Your mom might have something to say about that."

"She likes you. I know she does. Chris said he could tell, and so can Mikey and me."

"I like her, too, Danny, but when two people get married, there has to be more than liking. They have to have things in common, and—"

"What's that mean?"

Max lifted a shoulder in a half shrug. "That they like to do the same things, that they feel the same way about certain things in their lives, like how to bring up their children."

"Oh," Danny said. "I get it. You and mom both like baseball, and you write books and mom likes to read books. Does that count?"

"To some degree," Max said. "But there's more. They have to be able to look past each other's faults."

"I know about that," Danny told him. "Mom says I have to love Chris even though he bosses me around and thinks he's big. What else?"

"Lots of things," Max said. "But the most important thing for two people who want to be married is that they have to really love each other."

"The Bible says that," Danny told him. "In First Corinthesees, I think. 'The greatest of these is love.' That's what it says. Or something like that. And if it's in the Bible, it must be really important."

"It is," Max said.

"So you and my mom don't love each other."

What could he say? Even though he'd told Zoe just the day before that he wasn't ready for a new relationship, he couldn't deny he felt things for her that went beyond what his common sense told him he should be feeling. Instead of answering the question he was asked, Max said, "Your mom and I haven't known each other very long, and—"

"So you might start loving each other when you get

to know each other better, right?" he asked, a hopeful gleam in his eyes.

"There's always that possibility, I suppose," Max conceded. "But there's also the possibility that she'll meet someone else she'll love. Like Jack," he added.

"Jack!" Danny made a dismissive gesture. "Jack's a wimp." He said nothing else, and Max assumed Danny felt his assessment of the man who was going to have dinner at their house that very night said all that needed saying. Even though it was the opinion of a child, Max couldn't deny the relief that spread through him.

"What about you, Max?" Danny asked.

"What about me?"

"You could meet someone else, too. Someone that would keep you from loving my mom."

"I might." *But it's doubtful.*

A dejected look lurked in Danny's blue eyes. "I can still wish and hope you two will love each other, can't I?"

"Wishing and hoping for the things you want is always okay," Max assured him.

"All right, class," Mrs. Rogers said in a loud voice, ending one of the most stressful conversations Max could recall ever having. "It's time to go to the lunchroom. Remember, single file, no talking. Lara, you and your father lead the way."

Danny grabbed Max's hand again and smiled up at him. "You're gonna like the lunch. It's fried chicken. Sometimes we have mystery meat—that's what Chris calls it—but their chicken is really good. So are their rolls," he added as an afterthought.

Max and Danny followed the other children to the lunchroom. Feeling the warmth of Danny's hand in his, knowing he was doing something vitally important for the boy, Max couldn't deny that he felt like a father. Danny's father.

Chapter Nine

Max sat in the fancy Little Rock restaurant, as nervous as a kid on his first date. In a way, he supposed it was. Funny, he didn't remember feeling so insecure as a teenager. Nervous, maybe, but not so…vulnerable. Maybe it had something to do with having failed in the most important relationship of his life. Danielle seemed a little shy, too, even though they'd known each other for years. Max wondered if she dated much since the breakup of her marriage and if she was racked with the same self-doubts. Thank goodness his mother and Paul were there to keep the conversation afloat as they were doing now, while he enjoyed his prime rib and half listened to the ebb and flow of the conversation.

He glanced at the woman sitting next to him, her shoulders bare in a floral dress that had Class stamped all over it. Dani was exactly the type he always seemed

drawn to. She had a nice body, too—ripe curves in all
the right places, long legs and a tiny waist. In fact, she
was put together a lot like Cara. Dani looked like the
kind of woman who spent a lot of time at the gym doing
step aerobics and dancing with dumbbells and ankle
weights, again like Cara. The time she must put in paid
off. With her long dark hair and huge brown eyes, she
was a drop-dead gorgeous package. He put a mental *X*
in the plus column. As the evening progressed, he'd
been tallying up her pluses and minuses.

She raised her glass to take a sip of wine and smiled
at him, revealing teeth so perfectly straight they didn't
look quite real. He gave her a cursory smile back and
thought of Zoe's smile, with its slightly crooked front
tooth. He recalled the way her eyes crinkled, making
little lines fan out at their corners—laugh lines—and
the dimple that appeared like magic in her right cheek.

"—my job is the most important thing in my life at
this point," she said, catching Max's attention once
more. He lifted his glass to his lips and looked at her
over its rim. For some reason, her words set Max's
teeth on edge. He wondered if her ambition was part of
the reason for the failure of her marriage. Not that there
was anything wrong with wanting to get ahead, but
sometimes single-mindedness in one area was a detri-
ment in another. Having put his career ahead of his
marriage himself, he knew it was a dangerous road to
travel.

At least the night was clearing up one thing for him,
and he wasn't sure whether to be happy or alarmed by
the clarification. Though Dani was exactly the kind of
woman he usually fell for, she didn't raise his heart rate
one iota. He felt no sensation of confusion when she

smiled at him, no feeling of teetering at the edge of a cliff, no sense of being in over his head, no irritation at being aware of her beauty and brains—all the things he felt when he was in the same room with Zoe. Dani didn't make his palms sweat, his body throb with awareness. She didn't make him feel strong, yet at the same time vulnerable. Didn't make him feel smart and indispensable, the way he felt when Zoe and the boys asked him to do things for them.

He looked at his date's tanned shoulders and thought of creamy ivory flesh scattered with whiskey-colored freckles. Stared into Dani's dark brown eyes and recalled the intensity and teasing of an earnest blue gaze. Observed Dani's perfect body and thought of Zoe's slender willowy form, with its small breasts and long shapely legs. Comparing the two women was like comparing apples to oranges, unfair in every way, but he couldn't stop himself from doing it. The fact was, everything about Zoe interested him, from the way she dealt with her children to the way she gave so much of herself. Selfless. The word described her to a *T*. It wasn't the selflessness of martyrdom but of a truly giving spirit. She didn't do it to show off to anyone but because her family was truly important to her.

Money, though she needed it to survive, wasn't as crucial to her as the people in her life were. She had the talent to make good money with her art, yet she'd let her gift languish so she could be there for her kids. From his month-long observation, she seemed content to just pay her bills and be a good mother. Nothing wrong with that.

"What do you think, Max?"

The sound of his name brought his attention back to the room and the current conversation.

He gave a slight shake of his head. "Sorry," he said. "I wasn't paying attention. I was wondering how Annabelle was doing with Julie and Celia." *Liar.*

"We were talking about the latest round of interest cuts. Do you think it's going to stimulate the economy?"

"I hadn't really given it much thought," Max confessed. "I tend to stay wrapped up in my little fictitious world." He flashed the table his most charming smile and saw Dani's eyes widen a bit, in surprise, it seemed. "It's one of the hazards of being a writer."

"And what are some of the other hazards," Dani asked, leaning forward with genuine interest.

"You don't keep up with what's going on in the world or with your friends," he said. "You lose track of time and miss appointments. Your mind wanders when you're in polite company, working on a plot or a problem with characters. Writers are pretty much loners, which makes maintaining a relationship doubly hard."

As he spoke, Max wondered if he was trying to scare her off. And, as he spoke, he knew he was not only telling the truth, but seeing it for the first time. Writing held the inherent danger of becoming as consuming as the police work had. It was something he'd have to be careful of. He had to make sure he didn't lock himself in the cabin and do nothing but write. He recalled the string of things Chris, Mike and Danny had asked him to do since he'd moved and felt a smile tugging at the corner of his mouth. He didn't think there was much chance of the writing becoming an obsessing force as long as he lived at the cabin.

"Are you working on something now?" Dani asked.

"My second thriller," he said, nodding.

"Wonderful! Have you read the newest DeMille?" she asked of the group in general. As the conversation revolved around the plot of the book, Max let his mind wander again. He thought of Mike's request that he write him a book of his very own. Max fought the urge to laugh aloud. He knew nothing about writing kids' books. He didn't know much about writing for adults. He still hadn't gotten past the feeling that his newly found career was a fluke, that he was a big imposter, that someday soon someone would come along and tell him it was all a mistake and they wanted the money back.

"—there isn't much venture capitol money in the state," Dani was saying. Back to the economy again.

Venture... What kind of adventure could a kid Mike's age have? Max wondered. Maybe a kid a little older, like Chris's age, would be better, appeal to an older reading group. First things first. What kind of kid was he, and what could his name be? Sam? Nick? Nah. But something short and catchy and one syllable would be good, might capture a kid's attention. Ace? Now who would name their kid Ace?

What if Ace was a combination of his initials? Adam—which he thinks is a sissy name—Carpenter, which could be his mom's maiden name, Evans...Ace. Ace Evans, P.I. Not bad, Maxwell. Not bad. Of course, he'd be a lot like Mike—daring, adventure-loving, a bit aggressive and stubborn and with a heart as soft as a marshmallow.

The conversation flowed around him. Max did his best to be attentive, but he couldn't keep his thoughts from drifting to Ace and a plausible, exciting story line. Ace needed a sidekick, Max thought. Maybe a girl to pull in girl readers. He'd have to have a dog, some mongrel that no one else wanted, like Mutt. A dog and a crime. Dead bodies and drug deals gone bad for seven-to-twelve-year-olds wouldn't endear him to parents.

As often happened, a snippet of a scene came to him full-blown. His mind began to wander...

Ace looked at the girl. She was new in town, and pretty. Real pretty. Her hair was long and curly and sunshiny yellow, just like her name. Her eyes were as blue as the summer sky. She smiled, and he smiled back, thinking that she liked him. Unexpectedly, he thought of Bitsy and the way her red hair glowed like the embers of his Boy Scout campfire. Bits was his girl. Had been since kindergarten. More important, Bits was the only person—male or female—who could beat him up if she wanted to. And he figured she'd want to if she found out that Sunni Patterson had a crush on him. Course, the only reason Bitsy could whup him was because whenever she got mad his insides turned to mush, and all he could think about was making her smile at him again....

Zoe watched her dinner guest leave with a sigh of relief. Jack's divorce had been final since Valentine's Day, but even so, he didn't seem to be faring too well. She had invited him to dinner because she felt so sorry for him. She'd much rather have kept Annabelle. As it was, she'd barely been able to focus on Jack for wondering what was happening on Max's dinner date. Fortunately, Jack didn't seem to notice, or, if he did, he was too polite to say anything. The conversation at dinner had been pleasant, if a bit stilted. They'd talked about things happening at school, plans for summer vacations, the man who'd escaped from prison near Pine Bluff and their children. When Zoe mentioned that Chris was doing some pitching, Jack had immediately volunteered to help. Zoe had thanked him politely and told him that her tenant was doing that. Jack had looked a bit surprised and commented that the boys must like having a man around. Zoe concurred and refrained from adding that she liked it, too. Liked it too much, in fact.

Now, hours later, Zoe lay in her bed, Jack forgotten, unable to sleep for thinking about the near kiss. A soft breeze, carrying the essence of hyacinth, drifted in through the open window, moving over her like a lover's caress. She drew in an unsteady breath, savoring the scents of spring. It had rained that afternoon, one of those quick, springtime showers that left the earth smelling clean and new and green. When the clouds passed over, the sun had come out and set the raindrops shimmering on the leaves like miniature diamonds scattered about by an unseen hand. Even the singing of the birds seemed sweeter. Now, as she lay wooing sleep, the mournful song of a whip-poor-will seemed to mock the choice she'd made in pulling away from Max.

After having lain there for what seemed like hours, she finally heard the sound of his vehicle coming down the lane. Involuntarily, she glanced at the clock. Almost one-thirty. Rising on one elbow, she gave her pillow a hard punch and flipped it over to the cool side. It was a good thing he'd left Annabelle at Celia's. It would have been a crime to wake the poor little thing and drag her out at such an ungodly hour!

The headlights sliced through the darkness as he turned toward the rear of the house and headed toward the cabin. Zoe turned her head and watched the red glow of the taillights disappear and reappear as he maneuvered the SUV through the woods. She saw the lights go off, heard the car door slam through the open window.

Rolling to her back, Zoe stared up at the moon-dappled ceiling and imagined him going through his nighttime ritual. He'd go to his room and undress. She couldn't imagine him wearing pajamas. Did he sleep in his shorts or in the nude? She gave a little moan and closed her eyes, only to be assaulted by the disturbing image of a naked Max. Her fingers curled into the sheet that lay on top of her. Of course, she didn't know *exactly* what he would look like without his clothes. She'd seen him in shorts several times and once without his shirt, but she was a creative woman with a comprehensive knowledge of anatomy. Her imagination filled in the blanks quite nicely. She imagined him coming to her, crossing the room in the moonlight, taking her in his arms and pulling her close to his hard, warm body. For the first time since David's death, she found herself totally overtaken by the acute pain of an intense desire.

A sound outside the window, somewhere across the expanse of lawn that spread out between the house and the woods, banished the sudden unwanted hunger. Zoe lay stock-still in her solitary bed, her eyes wide, her ears straining to hear, her breathing almost nonexistent. There it was again!

Moving her head in slow increments, she turned to look out the window. Nothing moved in the soft glow of the moon, and she chided herself for feeling afraid, one emotion she hadn't experienced since moving into the house. Without warning, the memory of Jack telling her about the escaped convict flashed into her mind. Pine Bluff wasn't that nearby, but it was certainly within the realm of possibility that the man had managed to get this far.

Afraid to breathe, she turned to her side and reached for the telephone. Without even stopping to think of the wisdom of her actions, she dialed the number to the cabin.

There were no lights on in Zoe's house when Max drove by, not that he expected there to be at this hour of the morning. He was glad to be home, glad he'd survived the evening, whether or not it had been an actual date. Thanks to the fact that Dani was staying with his parents and was *almost* kin, Max had been spared the problem of whether he should try to kiss good-night, though he knew she wanted him to. He hadn't been on the shelf so long he'd forgotten how to pick up on those subtle ways women had of letting a man know they were interested. But instead of feeling good that a beautiful woman found him attractive, all he could think of was that he was extremely grateful she lived in Kansas. Thankfully, all that was expected of him was to brush a kiss to her cheek and tell her he enjoyed the evening.

Max parked the car and went inside, turning on the kitchen light long enough to get a drink of water before flipping it off and heading through the dark cabin to his room. He undressed and pulled on a pair of battered running shorts, contemplating whether he should turn on the computer for an hour or so. He couldn't get Ace's story out of his mind, but even though he was eager to put his ideas down, he knew that this was one premise that wouldn't be forgotten. There was too much of himself in it. It hadn't escaped him that Bitsy looked the way he imagined Zoe had looked at ten or eleven.

He was still lost in thoughts about Ace and Bitsy when the phone rang. Automatically, his gaze went to the clock. Too late for it to be anything but a wrong number or trouble. His first thought was Annabelle.

He answered on the second ring, barking a short, "Hello."

"Max?"

The voice little more than a whisper. "Zoe?" His knees went weak at the thought that something might be wrong with her, and he sank onto the edge of the bed. "What's wrong?"

"I hear someone outside," she told him in a low voice. "Outside my window." Fear quivered in her voice. "It sounds like they're in the edge of the woods."

Max leaped to his feet and went to the closet where he'd stashed his police weapon in a box on the top shelf. He took down the .9 mm Beretta—his and Martin Riggs's weapon of choice—and tucked it into the waistband of his shorts at the small of his back. "Ease out of the room and go to the back door. I'll be right there."

"Hurry."

The next thing Zoe knew, she was listening to the dial tone. She turned off the phone and rolled off the edge of the bed to the floor, crawling to the doorway. Once she was out the bedroom door, she rushed across the hall to check on the boys. Both rooms looked fine, and all three were sleeping soundly. As quietly as possible, she closed and locked their windows. Satisfied that they were all right, she raced along the polished wood floors through the den to the kitchen. She looked out the window that faced the cabin, but didn't seen any lights. Where was Max?

A light tapping at the back door sent her spinning around with a sharp gasp of terror. Max stood there, waiting to be let in. She hurried to the door, unlocked it and flung it open. Before he could step inside, she threw her arms around him and pressed her cheek against his bare chest. She felt his arms go around her, one around her shoulders, the other hand cupping the back of her head and pressing her close. She breathed in the scent of soap and warm male and knew nothing could hurt her.

"Are you all right?" he asked. His voice was a low, husky rumble beneath her ear.

She nodded and clung tighter. Then she tipped her head back to look at him. "Did you see anything?"

He shook his head. "I came along the driveway. I'll check the woods in a minute, but I wanted to make sure you were okay."

"I'm fine. Just scared."

"The boys?"

"Okay. I locked their windows."

"Good girl."

His hands gripped her shoulders to put some distance between them. Zoe's hands moved lower, albeit reluctantly. When she felt the cold steel at the small of his back, she stepped out of his grasp with near comic speed.

"You have a gun." It sounded like an accusation, and she supposed in a way it was.

"Of course, I have a gun," he told her. "I was a cop,

remember? You don't go into a potentially dangerous situation unprepared."

"I suppose not," she said, noticing for the first time that he wore nothing but a pair of faded, loose-fitting shorts and running shoes with no socks. He was very fit, without looking muscle-bound the way some of those guys on TV did. His shoulders were wide, his waist and hips narrow. Dark hair curled over his chest and down his hard stomach, a silky line that disappeared into the waistband of the disreputable shorts. Despite the fear she'd felt just moments before, she couldn't deny the hunger that surged inside her. Her earlier fantasies hadn't done him justice.

He shook his head. "You sure pick your moments, lady."

"What do you mean?"

"I mean don't look at me like that if you don't want to pay the consequences," he told her, a warning look in his dark eyes.

"H-how was I looking at you?"

"Like you're starving," he said bluntly. "For me."

She lifted her chin in a gesture of defiance. "You're dreaming, Murdock."

"Not at the moment, but I have been," he said. He turned the bolt so that the door would lock behind him, then lifted her chin with his forefinger and dropped a light kiss to her lips. It was nothing but the briefest touch of his lips to hers, but it felt as if her mouth had been touched with a glowing brand. She tried to think of some clever retort, but what came out was, "What was that?"

"That," he said, a corner of his mouth lifting in a mocking half smile, "was an appetizer." Without another word, he stepped through the door and pulled it shut, leaving a stunned Zoe standing there with her fingers pressed against her tingling lips.

His .9 mm at the ready, his mouth still burning from the touch of Zoe's lips, Max eased across the porch and down the steps, careful to stay in the shadows as much as possible. The moon was almost full; to someone trying to stay hidden, it looked as bright as sunlight. He moved from tree to tree toward the path that disappeared into the darkness of the trees. He was almost to the trail when he heard the rustling of brush and the snapping of a twig. He froze behind the relative cover afforded by a maple tree. Despite the fact that he'd been in situations like this countless times, his heart began to thud in fear. Anyone who claimed to have no fear was a walking dead man. It was fear that made your senses keener. Anxiety that made you move with caution instead of rushing into a situation you might not be able to control.

He waited for nearly a minute. When he didn't hear anything, he cautiously moved to the next place of protection. He counted to sixty and sprinted across the clearing to the path. It was much darker there, beneath the canopy of leaves. Darker and therefore easier for someone to hide. It would be next to impossible to see anyone unless he tripped over them.

There it was again! He pivoted sharply to his right, the automatic raised to chest level. Silence. Another twig snapping. Then, without warning, something darted from the woods across the trail. Again, Max spun, aiming toward the place he thought the intruder had crossed. Thankfully, the moonlight was sufficient

for him to see what was causing the ruckus. Relief
made his legs go weak. He lowered his weapon to his
side. A possum. He felt like laughing, but before he
could do more than offer a relieved smile to the darkness, he saw something coming at him from the corner
of his eye.

He didn't have time to do more than get his gun to
a half-raised position and pivot a half turn before something launched itself at him from the undergrowth. The
thing—it wasn't a person—hit his shoulder and sent
him staggering sideways. Something wet hit his cheek.
The second or two it took him to get his balance was
enough for him to take in new sensory information. Not
human. Bad breath. Friendly. Again, Max felt a profound relief surge through him.

"Mutt!" he said sternly, wiping dog slobber from his
face with the palm of his hand. "What are you doing
out here?" The answer to the question was obvious. The
dog, which Max believed to be an unlikely combination of St. Bernard and rottweiler, had most likely been
stalking the opossum. The dog quivered with excitement. He tried to raise up and put his paws on Max's
chest.

"No way," Max said, using his knee to discourage
the dog's intention. "You need to learn some manners."

Mutt gave a soft "whuff" of agreement.

"Come on," Max said, nestling his weapon at the
small of his back again and then grabbing the dog's collar. "Let's go back and tell Zoe you're the one who gave
her such a fright."

As Max approached the house, he saw that, contrary to his instructions, Zoe was waiting on the back
porch, not inside. His irritation evaporated at the sight

of her standing there in a shaft of moonlight that turned her auburn hair into a skein of pure copper. Her night-gown was something soft and white, scoop-neck and sleeveless, with tiny pearl buttons marching primly down the bodice. It looked old-fashioned and excruci-atingly feminine. He felt his groin tighten in apprecia-tion.

Bits was his girl. Bitsy. Zoe. Same thing. He loved Zoe the same way Ace loved Bitsy. The simple fact hit him with the force of a tidal wave, shattering his pre-conceived notions about another relationship on the rocky shores of reality. His heart began to beat a slow, sluggish rhythm. His stomach clenched with sudden nerves. He was scared to death, but he couldn't lie to himself any longer by pretending that what he felt for Zoe was nothing but sexual attraction. Couldn't pre-tend he wasn't jealous of Jack and even, God help him, David. Couldn't deny that he might want a permanent relationship with this woman at some time in the fu-ture....

"Well," she said softly. "What did you find?"

Max offered her a crooked smile. "Mutt chasing a possum."

Unaware or uncaring that he was the topic of discus-sion and that he'd almost given his mistress a heart at-tack, the culprit sat himself down in front of Zoe and nuzzled her hand, waiting to be petted.

"You're kidding," she said, scratching him behind his ears.

"I never kid about something as serious as an in-truder," he said, the smile gone now. "Roaming the woods is probably a favorite nocturnal pastime of his."

"I guess I heard him tonight because it's the first

night I've slept with my windows open." Zoe leaned over and caught the dog's head between her palms, unaware that the simple gesture afforded Max a shadowy glimpse of her breasts. "Don't you ever do that again," she scolded in a pseudogruff voice. Mutt's reply was to lick her hand.

"Mutt," she said, releasing her hold on him and wiping her hand on her gown. She took a deep breath, as if she were preparing herself for whatever was to come next and looked up at Max. "Thank you."

Max stepped closer. "My pleasure."

She gave a little shiver and crossed her arms across her breasts. "I'll probably never go to sleep now. Would you like to come in for a cola or something?"

He took another step. "I'll have the 'or something.'"

Something in his eyes caused her to take an involuntary step back. He reached out and grasped her upper arm with one hand. Her flesh was warm, soft. She looked up at him with an expression in her eyes that teetered between query and anticipation. He pulled her into his arms, none too gently, swallowing her gasp of surprise with a hard, hungry kiss.

He'd dreamed of kissing her for weeks, maybe since the first moment he'd seen her. There was something about her that spoke of wholesomeness and innocence. The girl next door. A good girl. Her candor challenged him, taunted him, as did the knowledge that she was naked beneath the pristine white gown. As any man would, he'd needed to see for himself if the fire he suspected smoldered beneath that demure demeanor. He wasn't sure what he expected from her. Hesitance, maybe, after the reluctance he'd sensed in her the day before. Indignation that he'd do such a thing. Righteous anger, even.

Instead, he felt no hesitance in her response. There was nothing but heat and a desperate sort of hunger that matched his. She's lifted herself on tiptoe and pressed against him from thigh to chest, twining her arms around his neck and threading her fingers through his hair to hold him close. They fit together perfectly, like spoons in a drawer, two pieces of a puzzle, as if they'd been fashioned exclusively for each other by God's own hand. Her body was warm and supple beneath his palms, her mouth equally so…hot, mobile, wet, welcoming each thrust of his tongue with a reciprocal parry, opening herself to him and all he had to offer.

He grasped the edge of her gown and inched it upward, his palm skimming over the smooth flesh of her hip to rest at her waist. Zoe's only response was a throaty sound resembling a sob. Reining in the desire that urged him to go faster, he drew away from her, lifting his mouth from hers, but barely.

Zoe's initial reaction to Max's drawing back was another little moan, a sound that ricocheted off his lips which were no more than a heartbeat away from hers. The groan pulsated between their mouths and drifted away on the breath of the night, a sound of denial, of desolation. Reluctantly, her hands moved from the back of his head to frame his lean cheeks. The whisker stubble felt rough against her palms, exciting in a way she didn't understand. His hand, still resting on her hipbone, was rough with calluses, exciting in a way she understood all too well. A few inches' movement was all it would take for her to lose herself in a way she suspected she'd never done before. The idea was heady, frightening.

"Okay?" he asked.

His breath fanned soft and sweet against her lips. She could feel them move as he formed the single questioning word. He wasn't asking if she was okay. He was asking permission. She moved her hand upward and let her fingertips trail over the line of his eyebrow. In the faint glow of the moon, she saw his eyes close and let her fingertips move downward, tracing the sweep of his eyelashes, the strong angle of his cheekbone and the masculine curve of his jaw. Her fingers moved to his mouth, lightly tracing over the line of his upper lip, letting her thumb graze the fullness of his lower lip, feeling its softness and the moistness she knew had resulted from their kisses, memorizing the shape of his mouth the way a blind person does, as if she might need to recall every curve and swell at some time in the future, knowing somehow it was imperative that she do so.

Certain she was about to burn all her bridges, Zoe couldn't stop herself from nodding. Couldn't have stopped the single, confirming action if her life had depended on it. And somehow, she couldn't shake the feeling that somehow her life did depend on her capitulation.

His mouth touched the corner of hers, one side, then the other. She felt the tip of his tongue trace the curve of her upper lip and delve into the crease of her mouth. She angled her head sideways, trying to capture his mouth with hers, to no avail. He was intent on lavishing her with soft, open-mouthed kisses that moved from her mouth to the line of her jaw, igniting small flames of desire wherever they touched, fanning the embers of a passion that had lain dormant for three long years.

She felt the tips of her breasts constrict to button

hardness, and yet, contrarily, they felt full, heavy and aching, similar somehow to the way they'd felt when she was nursing the boys. A sudden image of Max's mouth on her breasts rose in her mind, an aphrodisiac she didn't really need. But Max's mouth would give her no ease from the painful fullness; it would only stoke the hot fire of need that burned inside her.

She didn't stop to consider where this was all leading, didn't stop to reflect on whether it was right or wrong. For the first time in years, she pushed aside her fears, her worries, her analytical thoughts. This moment was solely about feeling his lips hot against the spot where her jaw and ear lobe met. The warm moistness as he directed those kisses to her ear, sending a tickling sensation throughout her body to settle in the very heart of her aching femininity…at precisely the same moment his hand moved.

Zoe gave a soft gasp, the only way she was able to get enough air. And then his mouth was on hers again, moving, tempting, persuading. But she needed no more persuading. Her mind was made up, her course set. She gave a shuddering sigh of acquiescence, letting her body go slack against his, feeling his hardness against her softness, male and female, yin and yang, positive and negative charges pulling them closer to a fusion of bodies, hearts and souls.

Again, he abandoned her lips. "Dear sweet heaven," he breathed against her mouth, "I want you."

Want, not love. At that moment, it didn't matter. At that moment, she could convince herself of the possibility that they were the same, though a still-sane portion of her brain knew the difference and cast the nagging detail aside. Want. She wanted him, too. Was crazy with wanting. Adrift on a dizzying sea of desire, aware that the feelings coursing through her could easily be shipwrecked on the sharp rocks of reality that lay ahead, all she could do was press closer, offering him what he wanted, what they both wanted…

"Where?" he asked, the sound of his voice intruding on the surreal emotions that ebbed and flowed around her. For a moment, she didn't understand, and then his meaning came to her in a rush. He was asking if she wanted to make love here or inside. Not inside! What if the boys woke up? It would never do for them to find Max in her bed.

She lifted an arm that seemed too heavy and pointed in the general direction of the gazebo. Without a word, Max swung her up into his arms. Hers circled his neck, and she dropped her head to his bare shoulder in a gesture of boneless surrender and consummate trust.

The trip to the gazebo was short, accompanied by the distant sound of a freight train, the sweet song of a whip-poor-will and the scent of hyacinth and jonquils carried on the soft breath of the night. Eyes closed, she imagined him crossing the yard, saw in her mind the twisted vines of the aged wisteria that shrouded the gazebo's interior, vines that would soon be heavy with clusters of purple grapelike flowers. She heard his rubber-soled shoes on the wooden steps, and, seconds later, felt him bend and lower her to the softness of the banquette cushion.

Elbow bent, her head resting on her forearm, her eyelids drifted up slowly. Max stood in front of her, his body a shadowy silhouette in the moon's silvery light. Even in the darkness, she saw the heat in his eyes, felt it emanating from him in almost palpable waves of longing. As she watched, he used the toe of one foot against the heel of the other to pry off his sneaker. Then, with no further fanfare, he unsnapped his shorts and stepped out of them.

He looked like a statue by Michelangelo—perfectly sculpted, achingly, uncompromisingly male—from the arrogant tilt of his head to his bare feet. Moonlight lay in slabs of silver across the flatness of his belly and gilded his wide shoulders. As she'd known, the softly curling mat of hair that covered his chest meandered downward across his hard stomach and beyond. She feasted on the sight of him, knowing it would never be enough to satisfy the hunger gnawing inside her, realizing that her earlier fantasies had deceived her. He was much more beautiful than she'd imagined.

He moved nearer and took her hand, pulling her to a standing position. Breathless, waiting, she stood immovable as he reached to gather the deep ruffle of her gown into his hands and drew it over her head. Then, naked and quivering with anticipation and nerves, she stepped closer and reached out to tangle her hands in the silky hair of his chest. She tipped her head back and looked up at him, wanting him more than she could ever imagine, waiting for some sign of encouragement.

"*Bon appetit,*" he said softly, and somehow, she made the connection to his earlier comment. The hunger he'd seen earlier was no doubt in her eyes.

...don't look at me like that if you don't want to pay the consequences. The sound of his earlier warning echoed through her mind. She looked hungry, he'd said, as if she were starving for him. And she was.

There were bound to be consequences. There always were. The difference was that she was walking into this with her eyes wide open. Consequences be hanged. This time, she was willing to pay them. Whatever they might be.

Chapter Ten

The soft dove-gray of predawn had softened the sharp edges of night. The sun would rise soon. What kind of day would it bring? Max wondered. He lay on the banquette, his head resting on one forearm. In her gown, Zoe lay beside him, her head tucked beneath his chin, the scent of her as sweet as the flowers blooming around the gazebo. His free hand was tangled in the fiery skein of her hair, his fingertips reveling in its silky texture. Her breath was soft against his chest. He knew now, firsthand, that there was indeed passion beneath Zoe's facade of wholesomeness. He knew now that one didn't necessarily preclude the other, just as he knew the wholesomeness—the goodness—in her was not concocted. As she gave her all to her children, she'd given her all to him.

Now that he was able to think coherently again, the

doubts were surfacing. He was willing to admit he was more than a little in love with her, which was something, considering he'd become highly skeptical about that ephemeral emotion's true existence. But what was she feeling? Last night, sharing the most intimate of acts, she'd been completely giving. Unbelievably creative. Filled with an unexpected fire. Innocently sexy— an oxymoron, he knew, but it fit, just the same. He had been humbled by her complete and willing surrender, but there had been no mention of love…from either of them. Were the emotions she'd shown him nothing but three long years of pent-up desire?

He'd never have believed it if anyone had told him there were degrees of satisfaction. Now he knew it was true. He'd never felt the depth of emotion he'd felt with Zoe. He was smart enough to know it wasn't the physical joining that made it special, it was something else. Some basic, elemental connection of emotions and hearts. Souls, maybe. Whatever it was, he'd never experienced it with another woman, and the implications terrified him. He didn't want to think of what more than just sex meant. Women like Zoe Barlow expected permanence, commitment, things he wasn't ready for.

In her sleep, Zoe drew a deep, shuddering sigh, the kind of sigh that went with tears. The hand threaded through her hair pulled her tighter to his chest. She had cried. Not much, but her eyes had been moist and a little sob had escaped her at the exact moment they had reached the summit of their desire. He'd felt it, too. It was almost as if the sensations spiraling throughout his body were too much to be borne. Pleasure so intense, it was almost pain. Emotion so pure, he'd wondered how it could exist in the barren place he called his heart.

Why had he felt so much? Why with this woman? Were the feelings and this love he thought he felt to be trusted, or should he do what all his instincts told him and run?

The little trembling sob awakened Zoe, but she didn't want to move. She was far too content to lie there and let her heart beat in perfect synchronization with Max's. It had been so long since she'd felt this way. Too long. Truthfully, had she ever felt just this way before? Satiated, yet still possessing a lingering hunger? Content, yet burdened with a nagging worry? Filled with a tentative hope, yet frightened to death? She'd never felt this uncertainty with David, but then, she'd known David far better than she knew Max. She'd known his intentions and that he loved her. All she knew about Max were the things she'd learned this past month, and of that, she knew little of his innermost feelings. What bits and pieces she did know had been garnered from watching him with the boys and Annabelle—only tidbits about his thoughts and feelings that she'd picked up from the way he dealt with her and her family. Her family.

Danny had gotten off the school bus the previous afternoon, grinning from ear to ear. Max had been great, he said. He was so glad he'd come. He'd eaten every bit of his lunch, so it must have been good, and he loved his shoe polisher. Zoe didn't know how Max really felt about the time he'd spent with Danny—she hadn't see him until he came to check out the intruder— but all that really mattered was how Danny perceived their time together. That time had been good for her son.

She also didn't know how Max felt about what had

just happened between them. Her own sense was that it had been good. Perfect. Everything she'd expected and more. He was demanding as a lover, but not selfish. Forceful, without forcing. Relentless in his quest for fulfillment, but determined that she be at his side every step of the way. And she had been. Her release had been mind-blowing, earth-shattering. Even now—who knew how long after?—she still felt weak, boneless. And she knew without a doubt that she did love him. Any lingering misgivings had been banished.

What about Max? His feelings would help dictate where they went from here. She'd never been in a situation like this before. She wasn't the type to indulge in an affair, which left what? Marriage? She gave a little movement of her head and felt Max's hand smoothing her hair, soothing her. Marriage was out of the question. At least for now. The problem was that Max had captured her boys' imaginations and their hearts because they were so hungry for a man in their lives. She was hungry for that, too, but she couldn't put their future happiness in jeopardy just because she wanted something—or someone. She'd had a good marriage, and she didn't want to follow it with one that might turn out to be a disaster, especially one where her children had so much at stake. They deserved better than that, and so did she. She could take the pain of a failed relationship. They couldn't, and they shouldn't have to.

Beneath her ear, she heard Max's strong heartbeat. His hand had moved from the back of her head to the place between her shoulder blades, his fingertips making small, concentric circles on her flesh. Of their own volition, her fingers began to do the same on his bare shoulder.

"Awake?" His voice was a deep rumble from his chest.

"Sort of." She lifted her head to look at him and saw nothing but tenderness in his eyes. Wondering if her fears were reflected in hers, she said, "Question."

"Yeah?"

"Exactly what happened here?" Her voice was soft and small and questioning.

His smile was crooked, with a hint of naughtiness. "If you have to ask, I must have done a bad job of it. I don't mind showing you again, though."

In spite of her worries, she had to smile. "You did a fine job, thank you, but I wouldn't mind if you showed me again."

Max drew her up his body until her lips were close his. "My pleasure."

"No," she said, as the space disappeared between their lips. "Mine."

Somehow, even making love a second time, she managed to get inside and into the shower before she heard the boys waking. She knew they'd head to the den to turn on the television, where they'd stay until hunger drove them to look for her. As she stood beneath the warm spray, the soft terry cloth moving with slow languor over her body, erasing every outward vestige of what happened between her and Max, her mind replayed every kiss, every touch. She would never forget the dominance yet gentleness of his possession. She would never forget him.

She donned her clothes, clipped back her damp hair and glanced at herself in the mirror. Did what happened between her and Max show in her eyes? There was a place along her jawline where his whiskers had rubbed, but other than that, she saw no outward signs of his loving. Thankfully, they were all inside, hidden, alongside the concerns that hadn't gone away or been answered before he left. She'd been dead set on getting some answers from him but somehow, she'd gotten sidetracked.

It hit her then, like the proverbial ton of bricks. She'd gotten sidetracked. Swept off her feet. Whatever you wanted to call it, her impetuousness had kept her from addressing a very serious concern: birth control. A hot flush of dismay swept through her. Somehow, she didn't think Max was the kind who slept around, and though she should, perhaps, be concerned with that topic, she wasn't worried. Protecting herself against an unwanted pregnancy was another thing altogether.

Concern dogging her footsteps, she went into the kitchen and checked the calendar, only to find that she was safe—hopefully. What would it be like to have Max's baby? Having any baby was a joy if the child's father was there with you and you were secure in his love the way she had been with her other children. Being alone would be an entirely different thing. And somehow, she knew that if the calendar lied and she did have Max's child, she'd be alone, simply because she wouldn't have the courage to tell him. She knew him well enough to know he would want to do what he considered the right thing, whether it really was the right thing for everyone concerned. Two wrongs had never made a right in her book.

She was pouring herself a cup of coffee when she heard a knock at the door. Zoe knew it was Celia, who came over almost ever Saturday morning while her family slept in. Celia was a sharp cookie. If anyone was likely to notice the changes in her, it would be her friend. Zoe went to the door and unlocked it.

"Hey!" Celia said with a smile as she pushed open the door. She held up her coffee mug. "I need a refill. Is the coffee made?"

"Hi," Zoe said, forcing a smile. "You know it is. Come on in."

Celia followed her into the kitchen. "Kids still asleep?"

Zoe rolled her eyes. "Are you kidding?"

"Everyone's still sleeping at my house, too, even Annabelle. But then, you know that. It's the same thing every weekend. Not that I'm complaining," Celia hastened to add.

"I know what you mean." Zoe poured her friend some coffee and set the sugar bowl and a spoon on the table. "How did Julie do with Annabelle?"

"Great. She's a good baby, and she went right to sleep in her playpen."

"Good. I started painting again." The statement came from out of the blue, and Zoe knew it was designed to keep Celia's mind off more personal matters.

"You did? When?"

"Monday or Tuesday, I think."

"What are you painting?"

"Annabelle," Zoe said. "The painting is in the den if you want to go see."

Celia did. Zoe was topping off their coffee when Celia returned. "It's wonderful, Zoe. And the picture of David is fantastic. I can't believe you've kept such a talent hidden."

"Thanks. I can't believe I gave it up when David died. Now I see that it would have been a good way for me to work through my feelings."

"Probably," Celia agreed. "So how are you and your gorgeous tenant getting along, anyway?"

That question came out of the blue, too, and threw Zoe for a loop. Her heart began to thunder. She strove for nonchalance and added a spoonful of sugar she didn't want into her coffee. "Fine." *Better than fine.* Hoping again to divert the conversation away from her and Max, she said, "He had a date last night."

"Really?"

"Well, it was Paul's niece, and they've known each other for years, but she's getting over a divorce, so who knows?" Her shrug said that was that.

"And how did your date with Jack go?" Celia asked.

"It wasn't a date," Zoe said. "I just asked him over as a friend. He's lonely and still crazy about his ex, from what I gather. I feel sorry for him."

"Time heals all wounds," Celia said. "When his are well, is he someone you could get serious about?"

"No." It came out more emphatically than she intended.

Celia held up a hand. "Okay, okay. Just asking."

"Sorry."

"What about Max?" Celia asked.

Zoe's pulse sped up again and she shot her friend a quick glance. "What about him?"

"Do you think he's over his ex?" she asked before taking a sip of her coffee.

Zoe stared down at the dark brew in her cup as she thought about that for a moment. Was he over Cara? It was hard to say. She chose her words carefully. "I think he's past the worst of the pain, and he may be over his feelings for her, but I think he has a ways to go before he's ready for another serious relationship."

"Hm. Tough guy like him, you'd think he'd just pick himself up dust himself off and move on," Celia said thoughtfully.

"Easier said than done, Ceil."

"I'm sure you're right." She gave a little shake of her head. "It's just that he seems so self-sufficient and just a little cool, as if nothing could ever touch him too deeply."

Cool? Max? Zoe knew differently. He was heat and fire, and he felt very deeply. The problem was, he had a hard time showing those feelings. She said as much to Celia, adding, "As a cop, he'd have to be careful not to let anything he was thinking and feeling show."

"You have a point," Celia conceded. "What happened to your jaw?"

Zoe's hand moved automatically to her face, while her mind raced to find an acceptable answer. "Oh, that. Something must have bitten me out in the yard. It's been itching."

"It looks like a whisker burn," Celia said in a dry tone.

Zoe's mind raced. If Celia even suspected there was anything between her and Max, she'd never hear the end of it. She considered and rejected a couple of replies and finally settled on an indignant "Good grief, Celia!"

"Well," Celia said, "it does look like a whisker burn. I was just wondering if your dinner with Jack wasn't a little more exciting than you let on."

Relief spread through Zoe like warm molasses. Why wouldn't Celia attribute the mark to Jack? She had no idea Max had been anywhere around the night before.

"Could you get serious about him?"

"I already said I couldn't."

"Not Jack, silly. Max."

"What brought that up?" Zoe asked, nerves spawning a sudden irritation. "We weren't even talking about Max. I swear, Celia, having a conversation with you is like doing the 'Who's On First' routine."

Celia stood there looking at her with a considering expression on her plump face. Finally she asked, "Do you know any Shakespeare?"

"Some," Zoe said. "Why?"

"Well, to misquote the dude, methinks you're protesting a bit too loudly."

"I didn't protest to anything," Zoe said, confused.

"Exactly."

After Max left Zoe's, he went home, set the alarm for nine and fell into bed, so exhausted he left the living room light on. He couldn't sleep for thinking of Zoe and wondering if she was as uncertain as he was about what had happened between them. When he finally drifted off to sleep, his last remembered thought was of her looking at him with tears in her eyes. The last sound he heard was of her softly crying out his name.

When the alarm went off at nine, Max rolled to his side with a groan, reaching out and shutting off the annoying bleeping. Even though he needed much more sleep, he had to get up, get showered and bring Annabelle home from Celia's. He didn't want to wear out her welcome, in case he needed to have Julie keep her again sometime. He drew a deep breath and tried to summon the energy to climb out of bed. The faintest scent of roses filled his nostrils. Zoe. Was she awake? Was she thinking of him? Did she have regrets? He swore softly, pushing aside the sheet and swinging his feet to the floor.

Minutes later, he stood beneath the stinging spray of the shower and scrubbed away the lingering scent of roses. Even though he was able to wash away the essence of her perfume, he could still recall its smell in his mind. Just as he'd feared, the willowy redhead was under his skin, had worked her way into his heart, and that was something he couldn't rid himself of with soap and water.

Why fight it? Why not just go with the flow and see what develops?

He knew what would develop. If he didn't end it quickly, he'd be pulled into a relationship he didn't think he was ready for.

He was toweling himself dry when a sudden thought brought a sharp curse to his lips. Protection. No, the lack of protection. He'd used nothing, because he'd had nothing with him. It hadn't even occurred to him. It had been years since he'd carried protection in his billfold, since before he and Cara married. He was surprised Zoe hadn't said something, surprised she hadn't stopped him.

Nothing short of a heart attack could have stopped you, Murdock. You wanted it too much, and so did she.

Stunned with the seriousness of the situation, he leaned against the bathroom sink and stared at himself in the mirror, seeing nothing but the image of him and Zoe together, their mouths and bodies fused into one, the sounds of their passion filling the dark void of the night. Dear God! What could he do about it now? Nothing. Common sense told him the chances of them getting caught were slim, yet the world was full of babies that had been conceived from a one-time encounter.

A baby. The possibility of a baby was a sobering thought, though it didn't frighten him as much as it might have a couple of months ago. Still, he wasn't hankering to become a father again. Damn! He couldn't believe he'd acted so irresponsibly. But he had, and he'd just have to deal with the fallout, whatever it might be.

Annabelle was glad to see him, and both Julie and Celia assured him that she'd been an angel and could stay any time. Unable to face Zoe just yet, he loaded Annabelle's things into the Expedition and drove to his mother's.

"You look exhausted," Donna said with concern. "Didn't you sleep when you got home?"

Max was thankful she hadn't been more specific. "I hadn't been home long when Zoe called. She thought she heard someone outside. By the time I checked it out and got home, I was too keyed up to sleep." *Actually, I was making wild, passionate love to my landlady, Mom.*

"Did you find anything?"

Max forced a wry smile. "Mutt. He was stalking a possum and making a fair amount of noise in the woods from time to time."

"Well, thank goodness it wasn't anything any more serious."

"Yeah."

"So how is it going?" his mother asked. "We've been out of town so much the past three weeks, and I didn't get a chance to ask you last night. Do you think it's going to work out?"

If I hadn't messed things up last night, there was a

definite possibility that it would work out. Now... "I'm not sure, Mom. Zoe's great with Annabelle, and the boys are as crazy about her as she is about them."

"Then what's the problem? I thought that's what you were looking for."

"It was. Is." Maybe the best way to handle the situation was to come clean. His mother had always been an expert at recognizing his lies, so why not tell her the truth—to a point.

"I don't understand."

"The boys have really taken a liking to me, and, I don't know...it's starting to be too much."

"What is?"

"They're always wanting me to go with them to do something or to fix something. Chris's baseball coach thought I was his dad and asked me to help him with his pitching. Mike wants me to write him a book, and Danny asked me to go to Dad's Day at school with him yesterday."

"Ah," Donna said with a nod. "I see. They've sort of made you their adoptive father."

"Yeah," Max said, nodding in agreement. "They're good boys, great kids, but...I'm starting to feel..."

"As if you're getting too involved in their lives?"

"Yeah. It's hard to say no. Don't get me wrong," he hastened to add, "I've enjoyed the things I've done with them." He smiled wryly. "I've even started jotting down some notes on a story for Mike. But Danny's teacher thought I was his stepdad, and...it seems like the more I agree to do, the deeper I'm getting in."

"And what about Zoe?"

"What about her?" he asked, his heart beating ninety to nothing.

"Are you getting in deeper with her, too?" his mother asked, genuine concern in her eyes.

Time to level with her...to a point. "I'm not going to lie to you. I didn't want to be, but I'm very attracted to her."

"There's nothing wrong with that, honey," Donna said with a smile. "She's certainly a special woman, if I'm any judge of character."

"I know there's nothing wrong with it, except that I don't want to be attracted to anyone at this point in my life. I just want to write my books, learn to be a good father to Annabelle and try to figure out what I did wrong the first time around."

"Don't be afraid to love again, Max," his mother said. "And I'm not talking about Zoe, necessarily. I do think you've learned a lot of things about yourself and where you went wrong in your marriage, and I don't believe you'll make those mistakes again. On the other hand, I understand very well how frightening it is to put your heart out there and take a chance on getting hurt again. I remember feeling a bit like that when I started dating Paul. But we can't dictate our feelings, and the heart has no conception of time. It just feels, and if its right, you'll know it, no matter who it is or how much time has passed." She winked at him. "Remember, you have good instincts."

Listening to her calm rationale quieted Max's fears, at least for the moment. If only he hadn't messed things up by making love to Zoe, he might actually feel comfortable pursuing a relationship with her...at a more leisurely pace. "How did you get so smart?" he asked.

"I'm not smart. I'm just old," she said, smiling.

"Be serious, Mom."

"All right. My take on wisdom is that we get smarter if we learn from our mistakes. It's sort of like what you told your Sunday school teacher when you were in the fourth grade."

"How on earth can you remember something I said so long ago?" he asked, amazed.

"I remember because it's so profound."

"I said something profound in the fourth grade?" Max asked with a cynical lift of one eyebrow.

"You most certainly did. Your teacher asked the class to give a definition of wisdom. One of the other kids said it was being smart. She told him that was close, but not exactly it. Then she told me that you raised your hand and said wisdom was knowing what to do with smart. There's a parallel here. Knowing what to do with smart is like learning from our mistakes."

"I've learned not to rush into things." *Yeah, but only after you rushed things last night.* "And I've learned that there has to be more than attraction and desire if a marriage is going to work. There has to be common values, something Cara and I didn't share."

"See?" Donna said. "You've come a long way the past nine months. And you've certainly come a long way with Annabelle, especially since you moved to the cabin."

"I have to admit the boys have been a help there. That and the fact that she doesn't seem so little and fragile anymore. I'm actually beginning to enjoy her. It's like Zoe said when I first called her. You do the best you can, and pray to God you haven't messed them up too badly."

"That's about all any of us can hope for," his mother said.

Chapter Eleven

Zoe was in the garden, picking lettuce for dinner when she heard Max's car coming down the lane. She tried to ignore the sudden racing of her heart, but didn't quite manage to. She wondered if he would stop, if she should stop him. Should she be cheerful or blase, or act as if nothing had happened? Maybe she would just try to gauge his feelings and follow his lead.

As the SUV neared, she reached up and brushed a willful strand of hair away from her face. The vehicle slowed, and she couldn't have kept herself from looking up for anything. He stopped a few feet from her, left the engine and air-conditioning running for Annabelle, who was asleep in her car seat, and got out, striding toward her with that loose, long-legged stride. Zoe, who was feeling a little inadequate at the moment since she was on her knees in the dirt, got to her feet and thrust her hands into the back pockets of her shorts.

Max was wearing jeans and an Hawaiian print shirt that was halfway unbuttoned, revealing the mat of curly dark hair that she knew firsthand was silky soft. He was wearing mirrored sunglasses so she couldn't see the expression in his eyes, which made assessing his mood that much harder.

"Hi," he said.

Zoe rocked to her tiptoes and back. "Hi." She glanced toward the car. "How did Annabelle and Julie get along?"

"Fine." No smile accompanied the comment.

"Good." The kernel of doubt inside her sprouted tendrils of despair. Her throat tightened suddenly, and she felt as if she might not be able to draw in enough air for sustenance. If their conversation so far was anything to go by, Max was suffering some postlovemaking qualms himself. The question was: what were they and how deep did they go?

He cleared his throat. "About last night…" His voice trailed away and he, too, stuck his hands into his back pockets. "It…"

…was wonderful. Perfect

"…shouldn't have happened."

Even though his words echoed her own sentiments, Zoe felt as if a knife had been plunged into her heart. "No. You're right," a cool voice that had to be her said. "It shouldn't have." Max didn't say anything, but she had the distinct impression that she'd shocked him a bit with her agreement. "Do something for me?"

He frowned, as if puzzled by her request. "Sure."

"Take off those dratted sunglasses, so I can see

your eyes." She was surprised at the tartness she heard in her voice, but he was ripping out her heart and the least he could do was have the courage to face her eye to eye.

Immediately, Max reached up and whipped off the glasses, folded the earpieces together and stuck them into his shirt pocket. The expression in his dark eyes was one of caution, with maybe just a hint of worry.

"Thank you." Seeing that her brief moment of defiance had gained the desired results, she gathered her meager courage and decided the best course of action was to take the offensive. "So," she said, taking her hands from her pockets and crossing her arms over her breasts. "Since we're in agreement on that, where do we go from here?"

"Where do you think we should go from here?" he asked.

What if she tossed a little guilt his way? "Since I didn't exactly expect last night, I have no idea what should happen next."

The comment had the desired effect. Guilt filled Max's eyes…and Zoe's heart for putting the blame so squarely on him.

"I take full responsibility," he told her. "I don't know why it happened, except that somehow you've gotten under my skin in a way no woman has for a long time."

"You make me sound like some kind of nasty rash," she quipped.

A brief, dry smile claimed his mouth. "No. Never nasty."

The admission went a long way toward softening her attitude, but she'd be darned if she let him know it. At least, not yet. "I want to make one thing clear. I didn't set out to seduce you or to get under your skin or whatever. I'm not some sex-starved, man-hungry widow looking for her next victim."

"I never thought you were," he said. "All you've done is be yourself. Maybe that's the problem."

"Meaning?"

"Meaning you're a very attractive woman, a warm, loving, caring person, and you've unstintingly shared those qualities with me and Annabelle. We needed that. But I read more into your actions than I should have. I admit that even though I'm a bit skeptical of the female population, I still have all the basic masculine needs." He exhaled an exasperated breath. "But having them and being able to deal with what goes along with them are two separate things."

Zoe shook her head and literally threw up her hands. "Never try to talk your way through an altercation with a wordsmith. Do you realize you've just admitted your guilt, pointed out my strengths and your weaknesses and implied you aren't able to deal with the consequences of your actions—all in a few perfectly executed sentences? What can I say to that?"

She turned around and started toward the house, fighting the tears that stung beneath her eyelids. She felt Max's hand close around her upper arm, felt herself being spun around. "Wait, damn it."

She tossed back her hair and glared up at him through tear-glazed eyes.

He swore softly and reached out a thumb to wipe away a droplet that clung to her lower lashes. "Don't cry, Zoe," he said softly, letting his hands rest on her shoulders. "Please don't cry."

She pressed her trembling lips together and gazed up

at him through a film of moisture, unable to reply without bursting into uncontrollable tears.

A crooked smile hiked one corner of his mouth. "For a wordsmith, I'm doing a very bad job of saying what I want to say."

"Just spit it out," she managed to get out through the tightness in her throat. "Don't try to pretty it up to spare my feelings." He nodded, and his hands massaged her shoulders gently. Despite herself, she felt the tenseness coiled inside her dissipating.

"I didn't plan last night, either. I've already told you I'm attracted to you, and my only defense is that you've been in my thoughts more than I ever could have imagined. I'm not going to deny that a good many of those thoughts have been sexual. Last night at dinner was no exception. All I could think of was you—" his lips quirked upward briefly "—and Mike's story. But mostly you. And when you called for me to come, and I saw you in that gown in the moonlight with your hair like molten fire…" He reached up and touched her hair with near reverence, then shook his head. "I don't know. You looked the way I imagined some sort of moon goddess might look, and I wanted you. Badly. My mistake was following through on that wanting."

"So you think it was a mistake, too?" she asked.

He nodded. "As far as timing goes, yes, because—"

"Because it's too soon after your divorce, and you're having trouble believing that your judgment is sound when it comes to the opposite sex," she said, interrupting him.

"That about sums it up."

"What do you want, Max?" she asked urgently, breaking free of his hold. "Guarantees that your next relationship will work? That there will be no heartache involved?"

"That would be nice."

"Well, good luck. I'd like to know I'll never make another mistake, too, but to my knowledge no relationship, no matter who's involved, is without risk of failure, or the risk of either giving or receiving pain. Life's a crap shoot. Win some. Lose some. Risk is an inherent part of loving someone, and if we aren't willing to take the risks, we don't deserve the rewards. And yes, since I see that question in your eyes, I'm including myself in that statement."

"So you aren't so sure last night was right, either."

"I agree that it shouldn't have happened, but I take my share of the responsibility. I could have said no. I should have, but I didn't. I'm human, too, and it's pretty clear that I wanted you as much as you wanted me." She forced a laugh, and it sounded bitter, even to her own ears. "Don't beat yourself up so badly. I've led a pretty sheltered existence the past few years, but I'm a big girl, and I still know how the game's played. I'm not naive enough to imagine there was any more to it than the obvious."

"That's what bothers me most. It might have turned into more, if I hadn't rushed things."

If possible, the fist around Zoe's heart squeezed tighter. It was too late to turn back the clock, no way to undo what was done. The only thing she could do was salvage what was left of her self-esteem.

Without acknowledging his comment, she rushed on. "You know, you aren't the only one hesitant about getting involved. I don't just have myself to think about. I have three children who are affected by my actions. I don't want to get embroiled in a relationship that will ultimately cause them pain." *Too late. Too late...*

Max only stood there, waiting for her to finish her tirade, his eyes dark with some emotion she couldn't read. "And you think I'd hurt them—and you?"

"I don't think you'd mean to, but you just admitted that you're not ready for another relationship, and they've already grown so attached to you that—even now—I think it's closer to a probability than a possibility."

"And you don't think this...attraction we feel might have grown into something more in time?" he asked.

"I'm not into guessing games," she said bluntly. "I'm more into reality. I've had to become that way to survive. What happened last night happened. All the talking in the world can't change it. All we can do is live with it and the consequences."

Max's face wore a look of resignation. "So you think we should just forget it happened."

"Forget? I doubt I can manage that, but I plan to do my darndest to go on as if it didn't happen. I don't want to lose you—" she paused "—as a tenant, and I'd like to keep baby-sitting for Annabelle."

He nodded. "I'm happy with our arrangement, too, and I want you to know that I'd never deliberately hurt your sons. Or you."

The regret in his eyes and the tenderness in his voice were her undoing. Her outrage and shame dissipated like fog in the morning sun, only to be replaced with a soul-deep sorrow. To get so close to happiness only to have it snatched away because of one moment's folly. "I know you wouldn't, Max," she told him in a soft voice. "I knew you could be trouble for us all the first day you came out here, but I figured my attraction to you was just a normal healthy response to a good-looking man. No big deal, right? So I took a chance that I could keep a lid on my feelings." She drew in a deep shuddering breath. "I was willing to take the chance. I knew that even though you might unwittingly hurt us, you would also give us something we really needed. A man in our lives. At the time, it seemed like a fair trade."

"And now?"

"And now I'm not so sure, but as I said, I can't take any of it back." She turned again and started to leave him, uncertain how much longer she could hold back her tears.

"Zoe!"

This time—thank goodness—he didn't touch her; he only called her name. She turned.

"One more thing, and then I'll let you go."

Don't let me go. Take me in your arms and tell me we can work things out together. "What?"

"Was last night a bad time?"

She might have imagined it, but she thought his face looked red. "Bad?"

"Unless you're on some kind of birth control, we didn't use any protection."

Zoe felt the heat of embarrassment flush her own face. Maybe she was naive. "I haven't had any reason to be on birth control."

"I didn't suppose so," he said, with a sort of fatality.

"Don't worry, Max. I should be fine."

"And you'd tell me if you weren't?

"Yes," she said, turning back toward the house and leaving him standing there. It was a lie, and she knew it. There was no way she could use an unwanted pregnancy to hold him.

Thank goodness Sunday was a day of respite. Max did his weekend chores, glad he didn't have to look at Zoe and feel the overwhelming guilt he'd experienced when they'd talked the previous afternoon. He told himself he shouldn't be feeling any guilt at all since she'd acted pretty offhand about it. He'd had her figured for the kind of woman who wouldn't go into a situation like that lightly, but surprisingly, she'd blown the whole thing off, as any woman of the world might do. He should be feeling good about the whole thing. Why didn't he?

Because of that look in her eyes.

Oh, she'd said all the things that should have made him feel better, but there had been those tears she'd tried so hard not to shed and that look in her eyes that reminded him of a puppy that had been kicked one time too many. He might not be the most sensitive man ever born, but he wasn't exactly stupid, either. The evidence didn't add up, and his guilt was rooted in the notion that she'd said the things he wanted to hear so he wouldn't feel pressured into making some sort of commitment. It was the kind of thing he'd expect from her, the kind of thing that made her so desirable.

A miserable week passed. Every day, Max took Annabelle to Zoe's in the mornings and picked her up about five. His book was going nowhere fast. He only had a couple of chapters to go, but he couldn't keep his mind on all the threads that needed tying up for thinking of Zoe. Things were getting worse between them.

Even the boys sensed something was wrong, asking if he was sick, or if he had PMS.

The only thing that got his mind off his latest problem was the story he was working on for Mike. He'd actually sat down and made an outline for a book. The only thing was, it might be too long for a kid Mike's age. Still, he was moving ahead and actually had the first chapter finished, despite the worries that plagued him and the deadline that loomed on his horizon. The book was one of the only bright spots in Max's week. When he'd told Mike he'd started the book, his first reaction had been, "What about your real book Max? Are you gonna get into trouble if you don't write it?"

A typical Zoe's child reaction. Max had assured him that he was fine, that he would finish on time, and he would—somehow. It was amazing how quickly the children's mystery was coming together, though. It was almost as if his brain had a direct connection to the keyboard. Even more surprising was his excitement as the story unfolded. Maybe his mom had been right. Maybe he could shop it around when he finished.

Mike was beside himself, too, waiting eagerly each day for the newest installment, which he insisted Max read to him and also insisted on taking to his mother to read. Max had given some thought to Zoe doing some cover illustrations as his mother had suggested, but he couldn't bring himself to ask her, since it would mean spending more time with her, a prospect both appealing and daunting. He had to regain his equilibrium. He didn't need anymore distractions.

Zoe, too, was having a hard time. The hours she spent with Annabelle were bittersweet, because she couldn't rid herself of the notion that her days with the baby were numbered. She knew she and Max couldn't go on the way they had been, and she didn't think he was at a point in his life where he was willing to make a commitment. She couldn't force him to admit feelings for her that he might not have, which left only one alternative—to go back to the life he'd had before he'd moved to the cabin.

When the boys asked her what was wrong, she claimed weariness. Truthfully, she was weary, an emotional tiredness that went beyond physical exhaustion. She'd waited so long to risk her heart and when she had, she'd gambled on a man that every instinct told her was not ready for the commitment she needed. Since the night in the gazebo, she'd done little but lie awake in bed, wondering why she'd been so stupid, why she'd let down her guard…wondering how she was going to live the rest of her life without Max in it, certain in her heart of hearts that that time was coming.

During the wee hours of morning when sleep could not be lured to her bed, Zoe found herself standing in front of the easel, painting. She had finished the portrait of Annabelle the night before last, and last night she had started sketching out some thumbnails for a scene from the book Max was writing for Mike. Mike had requested it, and the idea had stayed with her, so she'd decided to give it a try, based on Mike's description of the characters.

"Ace looks like me," Max said, "and Bitsy looks like an older Annabelle, except she has red hair like you, 'cause she has a temper. She's a tomboy, and he's real cool—sorta like *Happy Days* Fonzie."

Max was calling the book *Ace And The Cobras*. It

was about Ace and Bitsy figuring out that a gang of teenage thugs called the Cobras were the ones going through people's trash and stealing their credit card and checking account numbers, then using them to take money from ATM machines. Mike was thrilled, and Zoe admitted that the story was "grown-up" enough that even Chris seemed spellbound by it. So far, she'd come up with a couple of ideas for possible covers. The problem was, she couldn't let Mike know or he would tell Max, and he might feel obligated to use it if he decided to pursue publication, which, Mike said, he was thinking about, depending on how the story turned out. Though he was far from an impartial observer, Mike thought the book was fantastic, way cool. He'd been telling everyone at school about it, and they couldn't wait to read it. Poor Max.

Poor Max. All he'd wanted when he'd come to live here five weeks ago was a baby-sitter and a quiet place to work. What he got was a woman who'd fallen head over heels in love with him and his daughter and three boys who looked upon him as if he were some sort of god. No wonder Max was so leery of becoming involved. Would it make a difference if there were no boys in the picture? As she'd said time and again, a man would have to be a saint to want to hook up with her and her crew—and somehow she didn't think Max Murdoch was a candidate for sainthood.

Chris was a kid on a mission. He'd been practicing his changeup and wanted Max to see if it was going too high to be called a strike. He knew Max's stepfather was visiting, but it wouldn't take a minute for Max to watch and give his opinion. As he approached the back porch from the side of the house, he heard Paul say, "What do you mean you're thinking of moving back to the city? I thought you loved it out here."

Stunned by the question, Chris froze. From where he stood, he could see Paul and Max sitting on the back porch while Annabelle sat in her playpen, contentedly chewing on one of the skinny rabbit's ears.

"I thought it was ideal, but Zoe's boys are a bit more than I expected," Max said, running a hand through his hair. "They're always wanting me to do something for them."

"Like what?"

"I'm helping Chris with his pitching, writing a book for Mike, and going to school functions with Danny— who, by the way, told everyone I was his stepfather."

Chris felt tears prickling beneath his eyelids. Max didn't like them! They were being a bother to him, just like his mom said they would. Feeling his heart breaking into tiny pieces, Chris began to back up slowly. When he thought he was far enough that they wouldn't hear him, he turned and raced back to the path, running for all he was worth, running to get away from the things Max was saying about him and Mike and Danny, running away from the pain that clawed its way out.

"Correct me if I'm wrong, son, but I thought you said you were enjoying helping Chris."

The rabbit clenched in her teeth, Annabelle grabbed the mesh of the playpen and pulled herself to her feet. Then she took the wet rabbit from her mouth and threw it over the side. "Uh oh," she said.

Automatically, Max reached down to pick it up and

hand it back. "I am." He smiled at Annabelle and said, "Thank you."

"Ke ku," she said, smiling back and taking the rabbit.

"Your mother said you were having a blast with the Ace book."

"I am."

"And you told me you had a great time the day you had lunch at Danny's school."

"I did." Annabelle tossed the bunny again. Again, Max gave it back.

Paul's gaze probed Max's. "Then what's the problem?"

What could he say? That he was getting more involved with the Barlows than he wanted, more involved than he ever intended to get again? Instead of answering, Max swung his feet down from the porch rail and stood, looking out at the woods as if he might find some answers hidden beneath the tangled undergrowth.

"It's Zoe, isn't it?" Paul said. After a pause he added, "No. Not just Zoe, but all of them. You've fallen for her—"

Max turned to his stepfather and glared.

"—and without meaning or wanting to, you're becoming a part of their lives."

Max opened his mouth to say something, but Paul cut him off, pointing a finger at him and saying, "You don't like that, do you? It scares you to think that other people are becoming dependent on you—"

Annabelle pitched the rabbit again. Max picked it up. This time instead of handing it to her, he pried her fingers from the edge of the playpen, picked her up and sat her down on his lap. "I can't even take care of my own daughter, so, no, I don't want anyone else depending on me."

"You're afraid you might let them down, the same way you think you let down Cara."

"I did let Cara down," Max said, his voice rough with anger. Sensing his worsening mood and hearing the annoyance in his voice, Annabelle's lower lip began to tremble and she gave a loud wail.

"Maybe," Paul conceded, as Max automatically began comforting her. "But Cara let herself down, too. She wanted things all her way, and no relationship can survive happily if it's one-sided."

Max bounced Annabelle on his knee. "She claimed I wanted everything my way."

"You wanted to keep working at a job you loved. There's nothing wrong with that. And you did eventually give it up, so what did that accomplish? Your marriage failed, anyway. It doesn't make you a bad person. Stop hiding out in your make-believe world, and get on with your life."

Paul's accusation was like a slap in the face. Max stopped bouncing Annabelle, who, thankfully, had stopped crying. He lifted her to his shoulder and started patting her on the back in hopes she'd fall asleep. Is that what he'd been doing since Cara left? Hiding from life in the pages of his manuscript? The thought that Paul might be right was staggering in its implication. Annabelle raised her head from his shoulder and smiled at him.

"Is that what I'm doing?" he asked.

"Isn't it?" Paul said. "Granted, it's got to be a lot more comfortable there. You're in complete control of everything—from what the characters eat to whom they fall in love with, and the very best part is there's no chance of disappointing anyone or getting hurt yourself. That's no way for a real live person to live. If we close ourselves off to pain, we close ourselves off to pleasure, too."

Max knew Paul was right; he just didn't know how to fix it. He'd lived shut off from his emotions for so many months now, he felt paralyzed. Max put Annabelle back in the playpen.

"So what happened between you and Zoe?"

Max shot him a sharp look. "What makes you think anything happened?"

"You have a sort of lovelorn look."

"I'm not in love with Zoe."

"No one said you were," Paul pointed out. "But since you brought it up, maybe you'd better give the idea a little more consideration. But back to the boys. What do you plan to do about them? It sounds as if they've latched on to you because they need a father figure."

"I don't even know how to be a good father to my own child, much less to three boys whose real dad sounds about as perfect as a man could be without approaching sainthood."

"None of us knows how to be a good parent. We just muddle along the best we can and hope we can."

"Did you and Mom worry that you'd do something wrong? Max asked.

"Only every waking minute," Paul said with a wry smile. "Your mother's theory was that the mistakes would come out okay if you and Ryan knew we loved you and we were big enough to admit it when we were wrong or don't have the answers."

"Did it work?"

Paul smiled. "We think you and Ryan turned out okay. By the way, speaking of Cara, your mother said she could have sworn she saw her at the mall the other day, but before she could get close enough to be sure, she lost track of her somewhere in Penney's."

"There are lots of people running around who resemble other people," Max said, but despite himself, he felt a chill race through his veins.

"That's what I told her."

Dinner at the Barlows was a miserable ordeal. No one, including Zoe, was eating much, and she'd fixed one of their favorites: chicken-fried steak, mashed potatoes and field peas. As she stirred some peas into her mashed potatoes, she faced the fact that she was going to have to have another talk with Max. They couldn't go on like this. The chasm between them was growing daily, and it was beginning to affect the boys, who were usually disgustingly cheerful.

Tonight, they were all down, which was really unusual. Wondering what had happened to make them all so depressed, she said, "What's wrong, guys?"

Mike's lips twisted into a grimace and he stabbed his meat with his fork. "Nothing." Danny raised a despondent gaze to hers and looked as if he were about to burst into tears. Chris leaped to his feet, pushing his chair away from the table with so much force it crashed to the floor. Shocked, Zoe could only watch as he went running from the room. He hit the back screen door so hard it slammed into the wall of the house. Mike and Danny looked at her with fearful eyes, wondering how she would react to Chris's display of temper.

"You boys try to eat a little more," she said in a low

voice. "I'm going to see if I can find out what's wrong with Chris." She excused herself and headed for his favorite place down by the creek, hoping she'd find him there. Thankfully, she'd guessed right. He stood with his back to her, throwing rocks into the water—not skipping them as he usually did, but hurling them as hard as he could. He was angry. But more than that, he was hurting.

"Chris."

He whirled at the sound of her voice and just that quickly, the anger dissipated, his face crumpled, and he burst into tears.

Zoe rushed to him and pulled him close. "What is it, honey? What's happened?"

"It's Max," Chris said. pulling back to look up at her. "He doesn't want to have anything to do with us."

Zoe cradled his face with her hands. "Oh, Chris. That isn't so."

"It is!" he yelled. "I heard him telling Paul that he's thinking of moving back to town and that we were more than he bargained for and that we were always asking him to do things for us."

"Oh, honey! I tried to warn you about bothering him. He's a busy man, and he has a job to do just like a dad who goes to work somewhere."

"I know," Chris said, misery in his blue eyes. "We tried not to aggravate him except in the evenings and when we did ask him to do something with us, he didn't seem to mind."

"I'm sure he didn't. But I think his deadline is getting closer and maybe his book is getting harder or something, and he's feeling pressure. You know how I was when I was so worried about money."

Chris nodded.

"You know, Chris, I've told you that eavesdroppers never hear good things."

"I didn't mean to listen in. I just wanted him to see my changeup."

Zoe brushed back a lock of his dark hair. "I know your feelings are hurt, but try to look at it from Max's point of view. He's been through a hard time, and he isn't used to having kids around. He's only now getting used to dealing with Annabelle. The fact that he has been patient with you all says a lot about him, don't you think?"

"I guess."

"All grownups get tired of dealing with their responsibilities sometimes, just like you kids get tired of putting up with parents and their rules. We just have to be kind to each other and know that those feelings will pass. I'm sure the next time you see Max, he'll be just fine."

"I don't want to see him," Chris said, his voice quivering with the remnants of his anger and pain.

"Maybe you'll feel differently in a few days. Come on. Let's go back to the house. You need to eat something. I'm going to go have a talk with Max."

"About what?" Chris asked, his eyes wide.

Zoe tried to smile but feared she failed. She ruffled Chris's hair. "About lots of things," she said in a pseudocheerful voice. "About what we can to do make his stress go away. And that if he wants to move back to town, I'll be glad to give him his deposit back."

Zoe got the table cleared, the dishwasher loaded and the boys bathed. Then she sat them down in front of the television and told them she'd be back soon. Without bothering to freshen her makeup or tidy her hair, she set off toward the cabin, via the driveway, torn between her own misery and a growing anger at Max for hurting her children, albeit unwittingly.

As she stepped up onto the back porch, she heard the mournful sighing of violin strings. Max's mood matched hers. She took a deep breath and knocked loudly, hoping he would hear her over the sound of the music.

He did. He came to the kitchen door and stared at her through the mesh screen. Shirtless and wearing some low-slung shorts, he held a freshly bathed and smiling Annabelle in his arms. "Zoe!" he said, nearing the back door. "What are you doing here?"

She stepped aside so he could come out onto the porch. "We need to talk, Max. We can't go on like this. It isn't good for any of us."

"You're right," he said with a nod. His eyes looked as troubled as Zoe felt.

Annabelle leaned toward her, reaching for her. "Mama," she said.

Zoe's anxious gaze found Max's. "She hears the boys call me that," she said, hoping to explain.

He nodded and handed the baby to her. Annabelle twined her arms around Zoe's neck and pressed a wet kiss to her cheek. Zoe kissed her back, but she was looking at Max. "Chris overheard you talking to Paul this evening."

Max's eyes widened in surprise.

"He'd come over to show you his changeup," she explained. "He heard you tell Paul you were thinking about moving back to town."

Max nodded. "I've been thinking about a lot of things. That's one of them."

"He also heard you tell Paul they were more than you bargained for."

Max scraped a hand through his tousled hair and raised his gaze skyward. "Damn!"

"He told Mike and Danny," Zoe said softly. "They were all very hurt."

"I guess they would be," Max said, meeting her gaze head on. "I don't deny I said it, but it's too bad Chris didn't stay long enough to hear me tell Paul I enjoyed the things I did with them. One doesn't necessarily preclude the other."

"No," she agreed.

The sound of an approaching vehicle barely registered, but she did see Max's gaze flicker to a spot beyond her. "If you want to move back to town, I understand. Things have been a little...strained the past week."

"Yeah." He agreed, but his attention seemed focused on the approaching car. "Were you expecting someone?"

"No," she said, turning to look at the red Mustang coming down the lane. Whoever it was had terrible timing, Zoe thought. She needed to get things straight with Max so that she could have her life back. She watched the sporty car as it passed her house and headed toward the cabin. Even Annabelle seemed interested to see who the visitor might be. The car pulled to a stop a few feet from Max's Expedition. The door opened, and a pair of long shapely legs emerged seconds before a tall, stunningly gorgeous woman unfolded herself from the interior.

Even from where she stood, Zoe could tell the newcomer's eyes were as dark as the hair that curled down her back. She looked familiar, but before Zoe could place where she might have seen the woman, she heard Max say, "Cara! What in the sweet hell are you doing here?"

Chapter Twelve

Cara! Zoe knew her mouth had dropped open in surprise. If Max was shocked to see his ex-wife, it didn't show.

"How did you find me?" he asked.

"I hired a private investigator," she said. "It really wasn't too hard, since you weren't trying to hide."

"What are you doing here?" he asked again, wary concern in his eyes.

Cara glanced from him to Zoe, who held Annabelle on her hip. Ignoring his question, Cara said, "Aren't you going to introduce me to your…friend?" Zoe thought she saw a hint of uncertainty in Cara's eyes.

"Zoe, this is the former Mrs. Murdock. Cara, this is Zoe Barlow, my landlady. She looks after Annabelle while I work."

Cara's skeptical gaze examined Zoe from head to

toe. She wished she'd done something to make herself more presentable before she'd come to have it out with Max, not that she'd ever be able to compete with someone who looked like Cara Murdock.

"Nice to meet you, Mrs. Barlow," Max's ex said. "Thank you for taking care of my daughter."

"It's a pleasure," Zoe said truthfully, wishing she were anywhere but where she was.

"You're looking extremely well, Max," Cara said, her smoldering gaze moving over his body with a familiarity that caused Zoe's heart to ache. "How have you been?"

"I'm doing just fine, Cara, and you look wonderful…as usual."

Though Zoe couldn't read the expression in Max's eyes, the compliment seemed to perk Cara up a bit. She offered Max a tentative smile. "So, have you finished the latest book?"

She sounded genuinely interested, though for the life of her, Zoe couldn't see how Cara Murdock thought she could waltz back into Max's life after walking out and expect him to act as if nothing had happened. She was either very dense or very canny. Again, Zoe thought this should be a private conversation between Max and Cara.

"Why the sudden interest? You never cared before," Max asked.

"That isn't true. I just had other…issues back then."

"Yeah. And you settled them by walking out on me and our daughter." It was the first direct hit he'd aimed at her. Clearly, Max had run out of patience.

"I didn't settle them, Max. I ran from them. I realize that now." She shifted her gaze to Zoe and back to Max. "Look, could we talk inside? Privately?"

Zoe saw her chance for escape and took a step toward Max. No matter how contrite Cara Murdock seemed to be, Zoe couldn't bring herself to hand Annabelle to the woman who'd left her with a neighbor and walked out of her life.

"You said everything that needed saying in the letter you left the day you walked out."

"Please," Cara said, her voice trembling. "I've had a lot of time to think."

Zoe moved closer to Max. The only thing she saw in his eyes was a smoldering anger, held tightly in check. "You owe it to yourself and to Annabelle to hear what she has to say." She spoke softly, the words meant for him alone.

He looked down at her for long moments, as if he were trying to see into her very soul. Filled with her own confusion and fears, Zoe had no idea what he saw there. Finally, he took the baby from her. Zoe glanced at Cara as she passed, but went down the back steps without speaking. What could she say? Nice to meet you? Hardly. Cara Murdock's coming was just another obstacle in the many that separated Zoe and Max. Zoe heard Annabelle start to cry and hardened her heart to the sound. She couldn't take it. Not now.

As she covered the distance between the cabin and her house, Zoe forced herself to walk. She wanted to run, to hide, to let the tears that burned beneath her eyelids fall. She wanted to scream out that it wasn't fair that Cara had come back when she, Zoe, was engaged in her own battle for Max's heart. She didn't want to consider what might happen between Cara—who'd obviously had a change of heart—or to think about what her life would be like without Max. But she knew that probability was in her future, whether Cara was in Max's or not.

She entered the house and bypassed the den, calling out to the boys that she was home and going to take a shower. The last thing she wanted was to discuss Max with them. She needed some time to gather her thoughts and gain control of the fear battering at her heart and what remained of her fragile hope.

Max watched Zoe go and felt as if she were taking a part of him with her. Annabelle, too, seemed to know something was amiss, because she stretched out her arms toward Zoe and began to cry. Zoe didn't even look back.

"It seems Annabelle has gotten attached to Mrs. Barlow."

The sound of Cara's voice pulled Max roughly back to the moment. He was eager to get this talk over with. "She has." He moved to the door and held it open for his ex-wife. "Go on in."

She preceded him through the kitchen to the living-dining area, looking around with interest. Her smile was strained. "It looks like you, somehow. You never did seem to fit into our contemporary setting."

"It suits me for the moment," Max said. He gestured toward the chair sitting near the fireplace.

Instead of taking the chair, she said, "May I hold her for a moment?"

Max wanted to tell her no but knew a refusal would only add fat to the fire. He shrugged and turned Annabelle toward her mother. Cara smiled at the baby and held out her hands. "Come to Mommy, Annabelle," she said in a pleading tone.

Annabelle twisted her body as far toward Max as she could. The longing in Cara's eyes evaporated, and she let her arms fall to her sides. "She doesn't remember me."

"Did you really think she would?" Max said, recalling how quickly Annabelle had gone to Zoe the first day they'd come to the farm. He watched as Cara, obviously defeated by her baby daughter, sat down. He settled himself and Annabelle into a corner of the sofa and handed her a toy that was lying on one of the cushions. "What do you want, Cara?" he asked again.

"To talk."

"You never wanted to talk before."

She had the grace to look embarrassed. "I know. You might be surprised to know I've gotten some professional help, Max. It seems I was suffering from depression. It's very common after a woman has a baby, and it can sometimes last for a year or more."

"That's your excuse?" He knew the accusation was harsh, maybe even unfair, but at the moment, he didn't care. Selfishly perhaps, all he could think of was his total destruction in the wake of her letter, of the pain she'd caused him, how only in the past few weeks— thanks to Zoe—had he been able to move past that pain and insecurity and try to forge ahead with his life.

It came to him then, quietly, unexpectedly, that Zoe *had* taken a part of him with her when she left. She'd taken his heart. The realization was like a door opening, like being able to see clearly after being blind, like suddenly understanding all the mysteries of the universe. And he did. Love. As corny as he knew it must seem, love *was* a comprehensive cure for the ailments of the world. He felt the resentment and anger that had gripped his heart the past year melt away like snow on a sunny winter day.

"I don't have any excuses, Max," Cara said. "I'm just telling you what I know now."

Max knew that realizing the power of love made him responsible for its use. He chose his words carefully, wanting to make his case as clear as possible without turning their exchange into a free-for-all. "Depression may have been what finally motivated you to do something, but it had nothing to do with the feelings you were experiencing when you left. Our marriage was wrong, Cara. We're too dissimilar for it to ever have worked, and those differences go far beyond our preferences in decorating. I just wish you'd broken the news to me in a different way."

"You're right, and I'm truly sorry. I'm glad you see it, finally. I never wanted to hurt you or Annabelle the way I know I must have, but there were too many things happening that I wasn't equipped to handle. I felt as if I couldn't breathe, Max. I felt as if I were being smothered by all the things happening in my life." She clasped her hands in her lap. "Since we're in agreement that our marriage was over a long time ago, it leaves only Annabelle."

"What about Annabelle?"

"I made a mistake in leaving her, Max. She's the reason I came back. I want to take her with me back to California."

Max was surprised that he felt no anger at her suggestion, only a cold, fierce determination. "You did make a mistake in leaving her, Cara. A big one. But you may as well know that I'll never let you take her away from me."

Cara looked surprised by the vehemence in his tone, but she laughed, a sound that quivered with uncertainty. "You always were so melodramatic. It must be the creative juices."

"I like to think of it as meaning what I say."

"Look, Max," she said, a hint of anger surfacing for the first time. "There's no need to get nasty. I'm willing to let you see her a month or so a year, and—"

"Oh, *you're* willing, are you?" he said, his own anger on the rise. So much for good intentions and love conquering all. "Well, it might surprise you to know that when the judge granted my divorce on grounds of desertion, he also granted me full custody."

Cara seemed stunned. "You don't seem to understand, Max. She's part of me. I need her."

"You need?" Max shook his head. "You know, for a few minutes here you had me believing you that you'd really changed and had some insights into yourself. You haven't changed, Cara. You're still only interested in what you want, what you need. What about Annabelle and what she needs? Have you given any thought as to what's best for her? What happens if you take her and start feeling as if you're smothering again? Are you going to leave her with another stranger?"

Cara gasped at the blatant cruelty of his statement.

"Your actions don't sound so benign when they're put into words, do they? Did you worry about her at all while you were gone?"

Cara shook her head. "No. I knew you'd take care of her."

Max laughed, but the sound held no mirth. "Thanks for the compliment, but when you left her, I had no idea how to take care of her. I struggled. Emotionally. Physically. Mentally. I was scared to death every minute she was with me, afraid I'd do something wrong, something to hurt her."

Cara stared at him, looking angry and uncertain about what to say next.

"Let me make the situation very clear, Cara. You abandoned her. And I'm not giving her up. You say you've changed. If it's true, you'll do the decent thing and walk out of her life again."

Cara looked confused, as if she couldn't understand the turn the whole conversation had taken. "I thought you'd be glad to have me take her off your hands."

"You thought wrong." He cradled the baby's face between his palms. She smiled at him, and he smiled back, never loving her more than he did at that moment. "Annabelle and I have had a tough go of it, haven't we, sweet thing? But we're doing just fine now."

As he said the words, he realized they were true. He raised his gaze to Cara. "Go back to California. Meet a nice guy and have another baby. As far as I'm concerned, when you left this one, you gave up all rights to her."

Cara looked as if he'd slapped her. Her voice trembled with anger as she said, "You used to tell me that in your job you'd seen a lot of mothers who gave up their children because that was the best thing for them. You used to say you admired them for seeing that. Why is this different? Because you have a stake in it?"

"Those were mothers who were prostitutes or drug addicts, and the kids were living in a hell of the woman's making. In those cases, sure I was for it. This is different because you had every advantage. You didn't give Annabelle up for her sake. You did it for yours."

"I guess there isn't anything else to say, is there?"

"Nothing except for you to give me your promise that this is the end of it."

"So I get nothing?" she asked shrilly.

"You had everything and you threw it away."

Cara pressed her lips together to steady them. Tears filled her eyes and spilled down her cheeks. She reached out a trembling hand. "You have to give me something, Max!"

He didn't speak for several seconds. Finally, he nodded. "I'm not taking the hard line to hurt you, Cara. I'm doing it for Annabelle. Growing up is hard enough without feeling like a wishbone being pulled in two different ways. I promise you that when she's old enough, I'll tell her about you. I promise I will never say anything bad about you, and if and when she wants to meet you, I'll get in touch. I won't deprive her of knowing you, if that's what she wants. Take it or leave it, but it's the best I can do."

"You're not leaving me much choice in the matter." Cara looked up at him and whispered, "I'll take it."

Zoe opted for a bath instead of a shower. She'd been in no hurry, and since there was no balm for her bruised heart, she'd decided to settle for a soothing of her body. As she lay in a hot tub of bubbles, her head resting on a rolled up towel, the soft music of Giovanni playing in the background, she wondered what was happening at Max's. Was the gorgeous Cara casting a spell on him? Was she telling him how sorry she was for leaving him and that she wanted to try again? Zoe chided herself for her foolish thoughts. Whatever happened between Max and his former wife was none of her business. One glorious night in his arms didn't carry much weight in comparison to five years.

She felt tears squeeze from beneath her closed eyes and wondered how she could survive the loss of the second love of her life. And Max was that. Whether or not he was like David, whether or not it was the wise thing to do, whether or not he hurt her and her boys, as she feared he would, she loved Max. They all loved Max, even Mutt. Her few lingering doubts had banished the moment he'd told her that if Chris had stayed to listen, he'd have heard that Max had enjoyed being with them. They'd made their choice; they'd have to learn to live with the repercussions of that choice.

Cara's taillights had no more than disappeared down the lane when Max settled Annabelle on his shoulder and pushed through the back screen. He had a lot of things to settle, and he intended doing just that. He was tired of not sleeping, tired of the tension between him and Zoe. He was going to end it now, tonight, one way or the other.

When he knocked on the back door and got no answer, Max let himself in. He heard the television and followed the sound to the den. The boys were on the floor watching cartoons. Zoe was nowhere in sight. Just as well. This was between him and the boys.

"Hey, guys." At the sound of his voice, three sets of eyes were turned to him. Three sets of eyes with misery lurking in their depths. "Can we talk a minute?"

Wordlessly, Chris nodded, turned down the sound on the television and plopped onto the sofa. Mike sat up and leaned against a chair, his arms crossed. Danny sat on the floor, crosslegged. Laughing at the sight of the boys, Annabelle struggled to be free. When Max sat her on the floor, she made a beeline for Danny, who smiled in spite of himself.

Max focused on Chris. "I'm sorry you overheard me telling Paul those things," Max said.

"Did you mean them?" Chris asked, a hint of anger in his eyes.

"Do you mean that I said you were more than I bargained for? I said it, and it's true. I never expected to become so involved in your lives when I moved out here. I came because I needed someone loving and caring to look after Annabelle while I worked. I expected to sort of hide out here and write my book."

"What were you hiding from?" Danny asked as Annabelle pulled on a lock of his hair.

"Myself, I guess. My insecurities and weaknesses. The hurt I was feeling."

"You aren't weak. You're strong," Danny told him.

"Physically, maybe," Max said. "But I wasn't strong enough to handle the new responsibility of raising Annabelle."

"My mom said Annabelle's mom just left one day," Mike said.

"She did," Max acknowledged with a nod. "And sometimes that's harder to deal with than someone dying. It makes you aware of the things you did wrong, the things that maybe helped drive the other person away. You have to take a good hard look at yourself. Sometimes you don't like what you see, and you aren't sure how to fix it."

"What did you do wrong?" Chris, always ready with the hard questions, asked.

"I spent too much time working, and I didn't give her

the attention she needed. But the real reason she left was because she didn't love me the way she should. And I guess I didn't love her enough, either."

"If you didn't love her, why did you marry her?"

Max had only thought the cops were tough interrogators. Now he knew what it felt like to be on the other end of those hard questions. "I thought what I felt for her was love, but it wasn't the real, lasting kind. Love is tricky. It's easy to fall in love, harder to stay in love."

"Why?" Mike asked.

Max shifted his weight to one leg and raked a hand through his hair. "Because life gets in the way. You have jobs that might cause problems, you have bills, and you might have children when you aren't ready for them. Sometimes things that happen cause you grow into a different person than what you used to be. It's just hard.

"Anyway, I moved out here to be by myself and sort of keep my hurt inside, but you boys and your mom wouldn't let me. You came and you asked me to do things for you and with you, and I did them, and I enjoyed them. But at the same time, I was afraid that if I got too close to you, if I let myself care, I'd wind up getting hurt again, or I would somehow let you down, the way I had Annabelle's mother. I didn't want to get so involved in your lives that when I left, we'd all be hurt. But it's too late. I've gotten that involved. And that's what I meant by you being more than I bargained for."

"Why do you have to leave?" Mike asked.

"Yeah. Why can't you stay forever?"

"Because someday your mom will meet someone and fall in love with him, and you'll have a new stepfather, and you won't need me around."

Danny's face wore a look of disgust. "I *told* you that

we talked about you and Mom getting married, so *you* could be our stepfather. Why don't grown-ups ever listen to kids?"

Max couldn't help the small smile that claimed his lips. Yeah. Why didn't they? Kids had a knack for simplifying even the most difficult situations. "There's one problem with that."

"What?" Danny asked.

"Remember about love? The right kind of love? Your mom would have to love me and I'd have to love her, or it wouldn't work, no matter how much you boys might want it to."

"Well," Mike said. "Do you or don't you?"

Max plunged his hands into his pockets. "Do I or don't I what?"

Mike threw up his hands as if to say Max was a little slow catching on. "Love our Mom. You sure look at her like you do."

How to answer that? *How about truthfully, Murdock. Truth never hurts.* "As a matter of fact, I do love your mom."

"The right kind?" Mike pressed.

"Yeah," Chris said. "The kind that will last?"

"There aren't any guarantees," Max said, nodding, "but yes, I think I do."

"She loves you, too." Danny said matter-of-factly.

Max stood straighter. "What makes you say that?"

"She watches you when you go, like she doesn't want you to. And I've heard her crying a lot lately. Ever since the night the two of you slept out in the gazebo and you haven't been hanging around so much."

"What do you mean, they slept out in the gazebo?" Chris asked.

Max felt the heat of embarrassment creep into his face. He only hoped Danny hadn't seen more than sleeping.

Danny shrugged. "I woke up one night, and Mom wasn't in her room. She wasn't anywhere in the house, so I went outside. I saw Max and Mom asleep in the gazebo. Max had his arms around her and she was laying in front of him like spoons. I thought she must have had a bad dream, and I didn't want to wake them up, so I went back inside to bed."

Thank God for small favors.

"She's been crying a lot since then. I thought maybe it was because you had a fight or something."

"No. We didn't have a fight," Max told them. "But we do need to have a talk, I think. I need to find out if Danny's right. Where is she?"

"Taking a bath," Mike said. "But you can't go in there, or she'll yell at you. She doesn't like to be disturbed when she's taking a bath. She says it's the only time she has any peace and quiet."

"I'll take my chances," Max said. "Will you guys watch Annabelle for a few minutes?"

"Sure," Chris said. Max turned and started across the room. "Max."

Max turned. "Yeah, Chris?"

"If she says she loves you, are you gonna ask her to marry you?"

Max thought about the things his mother told him. When it was the real thing he would know, and this, he was sure, was the real thing, no matter how bad he might feel the timing might be. It was right, and he didn't want to waste another minute of living without Zoe by his side. He smiled. "Yeah, Chris, I am. Would that make you happy?"

Chris looked from Max to Mike and then Danny, the brilliance of his smile igniting reciprocal smiles on their faces. "Yeah, Max," he said. "That would make us real happy."

As Max strode down the hall toward Zoe's bedroom, he heard the poignant sighing of violins. He smiled. She was playing one of his favorite CDs. He stepped through the door and crossed the bedroom to the bathroom. The door was open, and he could see the foot of the long clawfoot tub that dominated the small room. Moving to the doorway, he paused and feasted on the sight before him.

Zoe lay in the tub, nothing showing for the bubbles but her head, which rested on a rolled-up towel. Even from where he stood, he could see the wet spikes of her eyelashes, a mute testimony to recent tears. Were those tears for him, as Danny claimed? Max felt something inside him fracture and knew without a doubt it was the last bit of the wall he'd built around his heart. Then, as it had the day Annabelle had smiled at him, he felt a strange swelling inside him—love, gratitude that he'd found her, and an overwhelming sense of unworthiness—things he'd never experienced before. This, then, was the real love he'd told the boys about. His boys. And he knew without a doubt that they were his now, his by virtue of his love. Another humbling, frightening position.

Suddenly, as if she felt the intensity of his gaze, Zoe looked up and he found himself staring into her troubled eyes.

"What are you doing here?" she asked, sitting straighter, but careful to shield her bareness from him.

"Loving you," he said.

"I beg your pardon," she said, her voice trembling.

"I said I was standing here, watching you, thinking of how grateful I am that I answered that newspaper ad, how lucky I am to have found you, and hoping you love me as much as I love you." Max heard the trembling in his own voice. He was laying his feelings on the line, opening up his heart to potential heartbreak.

"Cara?" The soft query held a multitude of questions.

"Gone. I don't think she'll be back. I made her see that leaving things as they are is the best thing for Annabelle and that I don't intend to give her up."

"I wouldn't think you would," Zoe said in a low voice.

"I talked to the boys about what Chris overheard."

"And?"

"And I told them that they were more than I bargained for. You're all more than I bargained for. I hadn't planned on falling for you all the way I have."

"Are you sure about this, Max?" Zoe asked, a frown puckering her forehead. "You have to be very sure. I don't think any of us will fare too well if you decide this is all a mistake."

"I'm more sure about this than I have been about anything in a long time, and the only mistake I've made is keeping you at arm's length this past week."

"Will you hand me that robe?" she asked, pointing to the terry cloth draped over a rose damask slipper chair. "I feel at a bit of a disadvantage here."

"That's my plan," he said, reaching for the robe. "Catch you unaware, ambush you in the tub and rob you of your clothes until you see things my way." He crossed to the bathtub and held the robe open above his head, giving her the privacy he knew she wanted. He heard the splashing sounds of her standing in the water and stepping out, felt her slip her arms into the robe.

"Thanks," she said, knotting the sash at her waist and turning to face him.

Max was still trying to gauge her feelings. She'd made little response one way or the other about his loving her and the boys. Still, she hadn't said she didn't feel anything for him, either. He hoped that was a good sign. He pushed a swath of damp auburn hair aside and rested his hands on her shoulders.

"I'm dying here," he said, his gaze boring into hers. "Can't you give me a little help?"

For the first time since he'd entered the room, she smiled...just a little. She rested her hands at his waist. "What did you have in mind? A little mouth-to-mouth resuscitation?"

Relief spread throughout him, leaving him weak at the knees. He felt one corner of his mouth crawl upward in a smile. "That would probably help," he said as she rose up on tiptoe, "a lot."

Their mouths touched in a kiss so soft and gentle it might have been the brush of an angel's wing. With a little groan, Max's arms slid around her, and he pulled her close, slanting his mouth across hers in a hard kiss of possession. He wanted to absorb her into himself, wanted her to be a part of him, physically, emotionally, spiritually.

It was long moments later that he ended the kiss. "I love you," he murmured against her mouth.

"Are you sure?" she asked again.

He pulled back and cradled her face in his palms. Nodded slowly. "God knows I didn't want to fall in love with you, but evidently, He's a lot wiser than I am."

"I didn't want to love you, either," she confessed. "I knew from the first day you came out here that you were trouble, that I was in trouble. I knew you could hurt me and the boys terribly, but I couldn't seem to stop myself from feeling the things you made me feel."

"Are you sure this is right for you?" he asked, like her, afraid of making another mistake. Afraid she'd think *she'd* made a mistake. "I'm not David."

"Believe me," she said, "I know that. I wouldn't want you to be. I've gotten sort of attached to you."

"Good. You may as well know that I've already talked to the boys about it taking the right kind of love for a marriage to work."

"Marriage?"

He smiled. "Oh, yeah. I guess I forgot to mention that I've already asked the boys for your hand. They gave me their blessing. In fact, they decided over a week ago that we should be married. They also think you should do some illustrations for the book, but that isn't nearly as important at this point in time."

Zoe tried to look put out, but the mischief in her eyes caused her pout to fail miserably. "Don't I have anything to say about this?"

"Sure you do," he said, dropping a kiss to her cheek. "You can say yes."

"Yes," she said, twining her arms around his neck and smiling up at him. "Yes, yes, yes!"

From somewhere in the vicinity of the bedroom door, a trio of giggles erupted.

"Told you so," Danny said.

"I said it first."

"No, I—"

"Da da ksss," Annabelle said and joined the laughter.

Epilogue

One year later:

So pregnant she felt ready to pop, Zoe sat at the drafting table in the room that had once housed the previous owner's castoffs and was now her art studio. She held a paintbrush in one hand and pressed the other to the small of her back.

"Honey, Joyce Kincannon is on the phone," Max said, poking his head through the partially open door. "Do you think you'll be finished with that cover art by the end of the week? They're really anxious to get it. Everyone is pumped for Ace's next book."

She looked up and smiled, but before she could answer her husband of one year, Chris appeared to stand beside Max. "Mom, Annabelle had an accident."

"I'll be there in a minute, Chris," she said. Then she

looked at Max with pleading in her eyes. "I know you hate it, but do you mind changing her? My back is really hurting."

"Hurting? As in labor-type hurting?" Max asked.

"Yeah," she said nodding. "I'm pretty sure this is it."

"Is your bag packed?" he asked, a hint of panic in his eyes.

"You packed it a month ago, remember?"

"Oh, yeah," Max said with a sheepish grin. Realizing he was still on the phone with his editor, he said, "I don't think the cover art will be there by Friday, Joyce. Zoe's in labor. Sorry. Yeah." He turned the phone off and looked at her in exasperation. "Why are you just sitting there, woman? Get a move on."

"You little rat!" Mike cried from the den. "I told you to leave my stuff alone! Mom! Danny's been messing with my model airplane!"

"Well, Mike ate all the chocolate chip cookies after you told him not to get any more!" Danny yelled back.

Her lips pressed together in pain, Zoe stood and arched her spine backward. The phone in Max's hand began playing "Take Me Out To The Ball Game."

"What?' he barked into the receiver. "Oh, hi, Ed," he said, raking a hand through his hair that was already standing on end. "Yeah, it looks like I'll finish Jeb III on time—barely. I don't care what you call it. Look can I call you back? Zoe's in labor and I— Good Lord, what in the world is that? No, Ed, I'm not talking to you," Max said, his horrified gaze fixed on Mutt, who was carrying something in his mouth. A rank scent filled the air.

"Mom!" Chris yelled. "Annabelle took off her dirty diaper and Mutt grabbed it."

"Ahg!" Max said, waving the air. "Put that down, you stupid dog. Ed, gotta go. *Now.*"

Max turned off the phone, grabbed the smelly diaper from the dog, taped it together as best he could and tossed it into the trash.

"Take this trash out, please," he said to Chris, who'd reappeared in the doorway, "and make that darned dog go outside. Who let him in, anyway?" Without waiting for an answer, he looked at Zoe. "We've just got to get him neutered."

Zoe smiled as a feeling of déjà vu swept over her. "Who, Chris?" she asked with a smile.

"Chris?" he said, dumbfounded. "I'm talking about the dog." He turned back to Chris. "Put your sister into the tub. Then call Celia and tell her to get over here, pronto. Your mom's going to have the baby."

"The baby?" Chris said. "Wow!"

"Mom's having the baby?" Mike said, running to the doorway, Danny close behind. Max turned to Mike and pointed a finger at him. "You're forbidden to watch TV tonight for disobeying your mom. Ditto to you Danny for not respecting your brother's things." Finger still pointed, he turned in the room, making sure he'd given all the orders he intended. His gaze fell on Zoe, the only one left. She stood leaning against the drafting table, laughing while tears ran down her cheeks.

"What?" Max's eyes were wide with concern as he crossed the room and pulled her into his arms. "Now don't go hysterical on me, honey. "I'll get you to the hospital on time, I promise."

She shook her head. and placed one hand against his whisker-stubbled cheek. "I love you."

"Well, I'm really glad to hear that since you're about

to have my baby, though as cranky as I've been lately I can't imagine why you do.

"Why?" she said. "Because you're my hero. Saint Max."

* * * * *

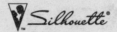

This December,

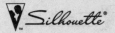

SPECIAL EDITION™

presents the emotional conclusion to

DARK SECRETS. OLD LIES. NEW LOVES.

THE HOMECOMING

by reader favorite

Gina Wilkins

Beautiful, sheltered Jessica Parks was determined to
rescue her mother from the mental asylum she'd been
imprisoned in years ago, but her controlling father was
equally intent on stopping her. Private investigator
Sam Fields had been hired to watch Jessica's every
move, and before long, she didn't mind having
those sexy green eyes zeroing in on her.
Could she turn his private investigation
into a personal affair?

Available at your favorite retail outlet.

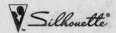

Coming December 2004 from

SPECIAL EDITION™

and reader favorite

Sharon De Vita

RIGHTFULLY HIS
SE#1656

Max McCallister had given Sophie the greatest gift—
the children her husband, his brother, hadn't been able
to give her. But not long after Max became sperm donor
and Sophie gave birth, his brother died. After years of
hiding his feelings for the woman he'd always secretly
loved, had the time finally come for Max to claim
what was rightfully his—Sophie and
his twin daughters?

Available at your favorite retail outlet.